Alice's fear re-forr

Anger that she'd been lied to. Anger that her son had been in danger.

She took a breath and unclenched her fists.

"Okay, if that's true, it's been six months since my son 'left.' Why is someone coming after me now? How would they even know about me?"

She saw Ben's lips tighten. He answered her second question first. "I think there's a mole somewhere in the police department. Someone exposed you to the gang."

The thought shocked her. She'd heard about bad cops, but she hadn't met any. Police officers weren't perfect. They were human and they could make mistakes, but this was something different. Knowing what they went through together, it would be a harsh betrayal if this was true.

"Who?" she asked. Not that she expected him to name anyone, but she'd like to know that this person was contained.

"It's not me, and that's as far as I can promise. It's my job now to keep you safe."

Anne Galbraith grew up in the cold in Canada but now lives on a sailboat in the Caribbean, where she writes stories about happy-ever-afters. She enjoys sailing the blue waters, exploring new countries and sharing her characters with anyone who will read them. She's been a daughter, sister, wife, mother, teacher, accountant, and is now thrilled to add author to that list.

Books by Anne Galbraith

Love Inspired Suspense

Kidnap Threat

Love Inspired Cold Case

Out of the Ashes

Visit the Author Profile page at Harlequin.com for more titles.

KIDNAP THREAT

ANNE GALBRAITH

LOVE INSPIRED SUSPENSE
INSPIRATIONAL ROMANCE

LOVE INSPIRED® SUSPENSE
INSPIRATIONAL ROMANCE

ISBN-13: 978-1-335-55459-8

Kidnap Threat

Copyright © 2021 by Kim Findlay

Recycling programs for this product may not exist in your area.

This is a work of fiction. Names, characters, places and incidents are either the product of the author's imagination or are used fictitiously. Any resemblance to actual persons, living or dead, businesses, companies, events or locales is entirely coincidental.

This edition published by arrangement with Harlequin Books S.A.

For questions and comments about the quality of this book, please contact us at CustomerService@Harlequin.com.

Love Inspired
22 Adelaide St. West, 40th Floor
Toronto, Ontario M5H 4E3, Canada
www.Harlequin.com

Printed in U.S.A.

The God of my rock; in him will I trust: he is my shield, and the horn of my salvation, my high tower, and my refuge, my saviour; thou savest me from violence.
—*2 Samuel* 22:3

For my mother.

ONE

Alice Benoit froze at the sound of glass shattering.

Her hands stilled on the cardboard box in front of her. There was a lot to clear out before she listed the house, and her neighbor Kristen had volunteered to help with her packing. In the back of her mind, she'd recognized the sound of tires on the driveway and had been waiting for a knock on the door. But Kristen would have waited to be let in. She wouldn't break a window.

Alice tried to reason the sound away. No one would break into her home. She was an ordinary person, and this was an ordinary morning. It couldn't really be anything bad. It must be an accident, a stone dislodged from…from… Her brain was flailing for an explanation.

Another part of her went straight to panic mode. *Run! Hide!* it shouted.

She was alone in the house. A widow of almost two years, she had been on her own since her son left on a university-sponsored expedition to the Antarctic six months ago. She lived in a rural area and always kept her doors locked when she was home. She'd married a cop when she was twenty, and for twenty-five years, he'd drilled safety habits into their daily routines.

She heard a male voice, one she didn't recognize, swearing. "You sure she's home?"

"Yeah, her car's in the garage."

The hair on her arms stood up. This was no accident.

Alice had no idea why anyone would be looking for her, but that didn't matter now. If these men had good intentions, they'd have knocked on the door, not broken in. She could hear more glass falling on the tile floor of the entrance, and she guessed the intruders were clearing out the remaining glass they'd broken to open the door. She had seconds.

Flight or fight? She had nothing here to fight with, but there was nowhere to run. She was trapped here on the second floor with only one set of stairs. Suddenly, she knew what to do. She had to get across the landing.

She tiptoed quickly to the door of the office. She peered around the doorframe into the hallway. No one was at the foot of the stairs. Yet. She heard the front door hit the wall. They'd entered the house without caution or fear.

The only safe place was in the master bedroom. She had to risk it. She took a breath and darted silently across the hall, breathing a prayer.

She made it through the doorway. Her heart slammed in her chest, and she shoved her hand against it, afraid it might be loud enough to betray her. She slid with her back against the wall, careful step by careful step, until she got to the closet. She listened for noise coming from the main floor and heard footsteps moving around. How long until they came upstairs?

The doors to the closet were closed, blocking the safety inside. As she reached out a hand, she heard a crash from downstairs. She flinched and forced herself to turn her back to the doorway, leaving her exposed and vulnerable. She had to get the closet door open. If she could just do it quietly...

She braced one hand on the sliding door and pushed it back gently. It stuck, snagging on something. She glanced back at the empty doorway and then pushed a little harder. With a jolt, it slid all the way open and rapped the far side. She paused again.

There was silence on the main floor. Had they heard her?

She slipped into the closet. This side was empty. Henry's clothes had always hung here, and she'd packed those up months ago. She slid the door back into place behind her and reached for the clasp on the side of the closet.

The hiding place was the result of a mistake Henry made when he'd renovated the upstairs. He hadn't measured the distances correctly, and there was a gap between the two closets. At first, she'd expected him to tear down one side and fix it, but he was a cop. He'd seen this as a possible safety asset, a hidey-hole.

The space was tight for storage, and Alice had been frustrated with him. But not now. Now, it could possibly save her. If she could just swing it open quietly... quietly and quickly.

She could hear footsteps coming up the stairs. Her hand was shaking as she brushed it over the wall. *There, there it is.* The catch was not readily noticeable, but she found it and swung the half door forward.

It wasn't the whole height or width of the wall, but it was enough for Alice to fit through. It had been years since anyone had been in here, but she didn't have time to check what the interior was like now. There would be dust, but hopefully that would be the worst of it. She had barely closed the hidden door again and shut herself into darkness when she heard someone enter the bedroom.

She hadn't had time to latch the hidey-hole door, so she crouched in the dark space, hanging onto the metal tab to hold the hidden door shut.

The sound of footsteps came closer, and someone slid the closet door back with enough force to make the frame reverberate.

The silence stretched forever, and Alice stopped breathing. Then the closet door slammed closed again. She heard drawers being thrown open and things falling on the floor. Then the footsteps crossed the hall. Alice slowly let out a long breath. She felt for the latch and used her fingers to mute the tiny click when it locked into place.

Neither the latch nor the door was designed to withstand any force, but having the latch closed still made her feel better. Safer. Her heart rate dropped. She slowly relaxed her crouch, so that she was sitting on the floor, staring at nothing. She was safe, temporarily.

Only temporarily, though. She needed help. Kristen was due to arrive soon. Alice had to warn her and make sure she didn't walk into this, whatever this was. Her phone was in her back pocket. She pulled it out, carefully muted the sound and started texting.

With the intruders upstairs, so close that she could hear them moving around in the next room, she didn't dare risk a call to 911. But she sent a text message to

Kristen, her closest neighbor, to warn her and ask her to get help.

Intruders in house. Call 911 ASAP. Stay away!

She considered the text for a moment and then added, Not joking.

She hit Send and pressed the screen against her chest, afraid the light might show through a crack if anyone looked in the closet again.

There was a slight vibration from the phone. She tensed, worried that minor sound might have revealed her refuge. She could hear the intruders in the office across the hall. She pulled the phone just far enough away to see the screen.

Hope not a joke. Called police. They're on the way.

Thank You, Lord, she prayed silently and waited, trying to tell by the muted noises if the intruders were returning for a more thorough search.

They were in the bedroom across the hall now. The voices were so close she almost jumped. They were on the other side of the wall that suddenly felt very flimsy.

"I thought you said she was here."

"I told you, the car is here. Where else would she be?"

"Maybe she left with someone else."

"There's a purse. Check that. She wouldn't have gone without her purse."

Alice grimaced. Her purse was there, with her wallet, all her ID, her bank and credit cards…

She heard the contents of her purse being dumped out. Her panic leaped to anger. What right did they have to go through her stuff? Adrenaline was pumping so loudly through her body she thought they might hear it.

There was a moment of silence, and then more swearing. She heard footsteps pound down the stairs. She tried to sense any vibrations from beyond the closet or to hear what was going on downstairs, but she didn't dare open the half door in case they'd returned silently, thinking they could trick her out of her hiding place.

She was prepared to stay here for a long time.

Her phone vibrated again.

Sirens just went by. You okay?

Alice's whole body went limp with relief as she texted, Yes.

Finally, she heard voices she recognized calling her name. She unlatched and pushed open the half door, scrambling stiffly out of the closet and into the bedroom.

It was a mess. The men, at least two, had managed to create a lot of havoc in a short time.

"I'm safe," she called as she bypassed the chaos and left the relative security of the bedroom. Two officers she recognized were at the foot of the stairs, looking relieved to see her on the landing in one piece. Toby and Dale. They were young, but they'd known Henry, and Alice had met them many times. They'd attended Henry's funeral.

"Sure you're okay?" Toby asked.

Alice nodded, starting to shake. She leaned against the wall, arms crossed, breathing in the comfort of feeling safe. It was reassuring to know that two armed men committed to serving and protecting the community were standing between her and the outside.

"The glass in your door was smashed. That's how they got in," Dale said.

Alice nodded again.

"They made a bit of a mess. Probably looking for something to steal." Toby scanned the room around him. His voice was reassuring.

Judging from what she could see up here from the landing, Alice could only imagine what the main floor must look like. But she didn't think the intruders had been here to steal. Not when she had heard them say they were looking for her. Not when they'd broken in after checking she was home.

Alice was about to explain just that when Toby got a call. He gave a wait signal with his hand to Dale and stepped aside. She and Dale stood, waiting silently. After a few moments, the call ended, and Toby returned to the foot of the stairs. He looked at her apologetically. "That was the acting super," he said, sounding a little surprised. "He's on his way here."

Ben Parsons steered his vehicle out of town en route to Alice Benoit's home. As soon as he hit the highway, he turned on the siren. He was anxious. Local cops were treating it as a simple robbery, but Ben knew it could be so much more.

The needle on the speedometer crept to the right as

his anxiety worked through to his feet. Fortunately, there hadn't been snow for a while, and the roads were bare. He knew Mrs. Benoit was with two police officers and the intruders had been scared off. What did he think could happen? After many years as a cop, his imagination could play a chilling reel of highlights.

Most of the people in the office of this rural detachment in Lychford assumed he'd been assigned from Toronto to cover a maternity leave. His numbers were getting up there. At forty-nine, his age plus years of service would soon reach the magic total where he could retire with a full pension. He'd joined the police force right out of school, so he was still relatively young, but he knew some of the higher-ups would expect him to want to retire.

Ben hadn't denied the retirement rumors circling him, but he didn't see it happening anytime soon. This wasn't a job for him. It was a vocation.

He was a good cop. That was all he'd ever wanted to be. He'd spent his career working in Toronto, and while it often hadn't been easy, he'd tried to make the world a better place each shift he'd pulled.

The real reason Ben had been sent to Lychford was to keep an eye on Alice Benoit on the Q.T. He'd been given the assignment because the pending retirement story was a good cover, and because people in Toronto knew they could depend on him.

Alice didn't know it, but her son, Chris, wasn't on a university expedition like she'd been told. He was a witness to a murder perpetrated by a high-level gang member. The whole force was invested in getting a guilty verdict. Alice's son was in witness protection until the trial.

The trial that began tomorrow.

Alice, the only family or loved one who could be manipulated to influence Chris's testimony, lived here, just a few miles out of town. She should be safe because the name of their witness had been kept secret, and therefore no one had any reason to know Alice was connected to the case. But Ben had been transferred here to keep an eye on her as an extra precaution.

The phone in his police vehicle rang as he told himself he was worried about nothing. The call wasn't coming from Alice's house or from the officers that had been sent out to respond to the call about a break-in. Neither was it coming from the police detachment in Lychford. It was a Toronto number. Ben knew what they were going to say before he even answered.

He listened to the voice on the other end telling him Chris had been shot coming out of a safe house. No one should have known where he was, or when he was leaving. If the gang had discovered that information about Chris, there was a big problem.

"The kid's all right?"

Getting an affirmative response from the other end, Ben's shoulders loosened two notches. There was still more than enough tension left.

"I have two of my men at his mom's house. There was a home invasion reported. The perps were scared off before they could get her. I'm on my way now. I'll bring her in myself to see the young man. Expect us at the hospital."

Ben's instincts were right. Things were happening. This hadn't been robbery.

Alice had gone through her story twice with Dale and Toby. They'd written down what she'd said, but she'd seen the skepticism on their faces.

Why would anyone be after her? She wished she knew. Alice offered a suggestion.

"Is there anyone Henry helped put away who could want revenge?"

She couldn't think of another reason anyone would break into her home to find her. Until this year, she'd been a high school English teacher. She might have pulled her own hair out a few times over some of the essays she'd had to mark, but she couldn't imagine any of her students coming after her for a poor English grade.

Her husband had been a cop. In movies, that was always a plot point. Had Henry helped put some powerful bad guy away for his crimes, and now they were out for revenge? It could happen in real life, couldn't it?

Dale and Toby looked at each other and shrugged. She sighed. She hoped the interim supervisor en route might be more inclined to believe her story. She knew the detachment supervisor and had been at the woman's baby shower, but all she knew about the guy covering her maternity leave was that his name was Ben Parsons.

When Henry was alive, before his heart attack, she'd known every officer in the detachment. Since his death, she'd avoided going into the station. She was out of the loop, and that might not be a good thing now.

The sound of wheels on gravel alerted her to another arrival. She tensed, but Toby looked out the window and announced it was the super. She relaxed again, resigned to the fact she was going to have to repeat the story of her eventful morning. She set down the coffee cup she'd been holding, her hands suddenly shaking again, and drew a long breath.

Toby met the new arrival at the door and gave him a quick update, so she had a chance to watch the man for a minute before he turned his head and met her gaze.

His eyes were a deep brown under frowning brows, and he scanned her quickly, then again more slowly, as if to reassure himself that she was unharmed.

Her first impression of Ben Parsons was that he was big. Not fat, not heavy, not any taller than Henry, but he was solid. Strong. He exuded an aura of calm, and she immediately felt safer having him here.

No wonder he'd been given this job.

For some reason, Alice suspected from his serious expression that he knew something about the morning she'd had. She didn't know what exactly he knew, but just as she was sure this hadn't been a simple attempted robbery, she was sure he knew something about why those men had been in her house.

She shivered as a chill dropped down her spine. This man, strong or not, was bringing trouble with him.

The pictures didn't do her justice, Ben thought. Standing in the entrance to a hallway covered with broken glass, he had a moment to examine the woman he'd been sent to watch over.

Alice Benoit was good-looking, even mussed up and shocked.

Ben shook himself mentally. Not the time or place. Not ever the time or place.

Toby had given him a quick rundown of Alice's story. Toby was skeptical, but Ben knew Alice was right. The men had been looking for her.

He could tell Toby the real reason someone was after Alice, but this was still officially a covert operation, despite the obvious leak that had resulted in Chris's shooting and the break-in here. He needed to keep the information as private as possible, and he had no authorization to reveal any of his knowledge to anyone but Alice Benoit.

He glanced back at her. She was watching him, waiting for something from him.

He considered sending Dale and Toby on their way so he could tell her what was going on with her son. Then he could take her in to Lychford, switch vehicles and get her to the hospital in Toronto. He decided against that.

The people who were after her would not give up. They may have been temporarily thwarted, but they'd be waiting for another chance. If they saw Dale and Toby leave, they might return. With reinforcements. That would leave only Ben to protect her, which was not a risk he was willing to take.

He needed to get her to Toronto, ASAP. But he didn't want to take his cop vehicle. He couldn't prove it, but he suspected someone in the Toronto Police Department was revealing this information.

If there was a mole, they might have access to information like his plates and possibly even his vehicle's GPS location. He considered his options.

They needed to take her to the detachment, where Ben could get updated information and they could head to Toronto with proper security. Maybe by that point they'd know for sure if someone on the inside was spilling information.

Now, how best to accomplish this without Dale and Toby getting suspicious? It wasn't standard operating procedure to take a home-invasion victim in. However…

"Mrs. Benoit, I'm Ben Parsons. Toby told me what happened here and that you think this could be connected to your late husband. Would you mind coming into the detachment with my officers and filling out an official report? Then we can look into some of your husband's old cases, see if anyone he helped incarcerate might be looking to get some revenge. They might not be aware your husband has passed."

He could see the surprise on Dale and Toby's faces and the comprehension on hers.

He felt a surge of admiration for her intelligence. She accepted his suggestion at face value, but he could tell she knew there was more to it. She didn't say so. That would make this a little easier to pull off.

His phone rang. Toronto again.

He clicked on the call button. "Give me two minutes." He slipped the phone back into his pocket so no one could see who was calling.

"Officers, you take Mrs. Benoit in your vehicle to the office and get her report. Mrs. Benoit, if you'll give me your keys, I'll lock up."

Alice's teeth were chewing her bottom lip. "Unfortunately, as I told Toby and Dale when we went through the house, the thieves took my keys, as well as most of the contents of my purse. I don't think there's much left for anyone to steal, so if you'll just close the door?"

Ben nodded, watching her carefully, knowing she was going to be upset by the information he had for her.

Alice asked to go upstairs to get what remained of her purse and its contents. Back on the main floor, she grabbed a jacket and pulled on her boots. Ben noted her pallor. She was in shock.

"Turn the heat up in the car," he said under his breath to Dale.

Ben watched them get in the cruiser, and after he got in his own vehicle, he put his phone back to his ear. He listened to the caller and pulled out of the driveway a few moments after the officers and Mrs. Benoit.

"Can you repeat that?"

TWO

Alice sent a reassuring text to Kristen as they passed her friend's house. She was grateful that Kristen had called and gotten such a rapid response. Alice had felt menace in the presence of those men. Something big was going on, and she needed to talk to the acting super, Ben Parsons. He knew what it was.

Dale was at the wheel, and to fill in the time, Toby turned around in his seat and started to tell her about his wedding plans. He was getting married that summer to someone Alice knew from their church.

"So Monica is having problems getting the right colors for the tables. She says they've got peach napkins, but our color is apricot. To me, it's all orange—"

Dale suddenly broke in, his eyes on the rearview mirror.

"What's with the truck behind us?"

Toby and Alice turned to look. A big SUV was closing in on them fast. Too fast. If the driver didn't slow down...

Toby yelled, "Get down!" He was reaching for the radio when the first impact hit.

The SUV crashed into their back bumper, and the car surged forward. Dale fought to control the car. They were rammed again, this time from the left side as the aggressive SUV came up the middle of the highway behind them. Alice ducked as the police car swerved and headed sideways.

Toby had the radio in his hand to call for help, but it was too late. Dale lost control of the car as a third terrifying impact sent them spinning into the ditch.

Time slowed. A confused kaleidoscope of impressions made Alice dizzy. She was jammed into the footwell in the back seat. The car spun, bumped over rough ground and stopped abruptly. She heard Toby call to Dale, but there was no answer. He started to call on the radio again when a gunshot rang out.

Alice could do nothing but pray, so she prayed as never before. Before today, she'd never been in physical danger. The reality of it was different than she'd imagined from watching TV shows and movies. She couldn't think clearly. Her brain couldn't focus on anything other than staying alive. She internally chanted, over and over, *Help me, Lord!*

There were more gunshots. Toby opened his door. Alice wanted to yell at him to stay safe inside, but a bullet shattered the window, passed by her head and imbedded itself in the seat where Toby had been seconds before. Glass from the car window sprinkled over the seat she'd occupied moments ago. Her adrenaline spiked, urging her to action.

She heard a shot from Toby's weapon, mere inches away from her, then more in return and a sudden yelp of pain. Her prayers intensified.

Suddenly, blessedly, there was the sound of a siren. No more gunshots. She heard the screech of tires, presumably the attacking vehicle speeding away, while the siren sound came to a halt beside them. She'd never heard anything so wonderful.

Arms trembling, she pushed herself up from the floor.

Ben frowned as he pulled onto the highway, leaving the Benoit home. Indulging his anxiety, he turned on his siren again. Better safe than sorry. That gut feeling, the one telling him something was wrong, was back in full force.

The man Alice's son was going to testify against was head of what Ben considered to be the worst gang in Toronto. He was willing to cross any line, inflict any amount of pain in pursuit of his goals. Currently, his goal was to stay out of prison.

And all that stood between him and freedom was a university kid. Since their attack on Chris had failed, their only chance to muzzle him was the kid's mother.

Ben turned a corner at a speed that was just this side of safe, and what he saw justified every concern he'd had. The police car transporting Mrs. Benoit was tilted at a crazy angle in the ditch. One officer, Toby, was outside the car, aiming his weapon at two men in an SUV pulled up behind the squad car. Toby's gun wavered, and Ben realized he was hurt. Adrenaline pumped through Ben's veins as his foot came off the gas.

He had a choice. He could follow the fleeing SUV or stop to check on his men and Alice.

He made his decision and braked hard, fighting

to hold his own vehicle under control while the tires screamed in protest. The back end swung wide, but he kept it on the pavement and came to a shuddering halt by the damaged patrol car. Ben saw a woman sitting up in the back of the police car. They hadn't got her. A weight dropped off his shoulders, and he relaxed his tight grip on the steering wheel.

Toby collapsed against the side of the car. Ben could now see red dripping from the arm the young man was holding with his opposite hand.

Ben quickly called in the accident to dispatch and described the escaping vehicle. He hadn't gotten close enough to get a plate, but they'd get all units on the lookout for it. Then he jumped from his vehicle to see how bad the situation was.

He slid down the snowbank to where the battered cruiser was tilted at an awkward angle. While Toby was outside the car, Dale was slumped over the wheel.

Ben checked Dale for a pulse. It was there, steady and strong. Another wave of relief hit him.

"What happened?"

Toby shook his head. "Sorry, sir." He panted. "They came up out of nowhere, got behind us and rammed us. We weren't expecting—"

Ben clenched his jaw. He should have warned the guys, even though he wasn't supposed to tell anyone what was going on with Alice Benoit. He also should have stuck closer to them instead of hanging back while he took the call. That was on him. Safe to say secrecy wasn't an option any longer. He'd do his best to keep the lid on, but his men would need to know what they were facing. It was his job to deal with the situation in front of him now.

"Not your fault, Toby. What happened after they ran you off the road?"

Ben examined the wound on Toby's arm while he talked. Fortunately, it was just a flesh wound, though it was deep enough to bleed and handicap him in a gunfight.

"One guy jumped out with a handgun. He had a balaclava on, so I couldn't see much of him. I was on my own, 'cause Dale hit his head and was knocked out when the car went into the ditch. I got my weapon out, but he winged me before I got more than one shot off. The other guy started this way, but then we heard you coming—"

Ben looked to the front seat of the car. Dale was starting to groan, so that was one concern abated. He nodded to Toby for him to tend to his partner and turned his gaze to the back seat, where he found Alice Benoit staring at him with a wary expression.

Ben forced open the door and gestured for her to come out. She hesitated, then slid her legs out and stood up cautiously.

"Are you okay, Mrs. Benoit?"

Her hair was disheveled, and her face was pale. Her clothes were dusty and covered with fragments of glass, but there was no blood. She was shaky but appeared to be hanging on to her composure. She'd just been through two attempted abductions and could be excused for being upset, hysterical even. He'd seen a lot of reactions over the years while dealing with people going through their worst circumstances, both men and women.

"No bones broken. No bullet wounds," she said. He could see her hands trembling in her gloves before she thrust them into her pockets. He admired her courage and self-control. It was going to help. He needed to get her to Toronto now, and it would make things a whole lot easier if he could concentrate on doing that rather than on needing to reassure her.

There was no longer any chance of getting to the detachment first.

When he didn't respond immediately, she said, "After two attacks, that's the best you're going to get, Superintendent." There was a sharp edge to her voice.

Ben knew she'd a teacher. The tone in her voice reminded him of some of the teachers he'd had years ago who'd warned him when he was about to cross a line. His lips twitched. "I appreciate that. I think we're all grateful things aren't worse right now."

After another quick scan to make sure she really was physically unharmed, he turned to Toby. "I've got a couple of cars and an ambulance coming. Will you be okay?"

Toby grimaced but nodded. "Dale is coming to. My arm hurts, but it's just a graze. You think those guys will come back?"

Ben frowned. "It's possible. I need to get Mrs. Benoit out of here in case they do."

Toby blanched but straightened. Dale had finally regained full consciousness and was asking what was going on.

Ben heard the faint sound of sirens.

He turned to his constables. "I hear help coming, so I'm taking Mrs. Benoit. Make sure that arm is dealt with, as well as Dale's head. I'll be in touch when I can. If anyone asks, I'm making sure Mrs. Benoit is safe. Don't tell them anything else."

Toby frowned. "Are you taking her to the detachment?"

"I'm keeping her safe," Ben repeated and turned from Toby's bewildered gaze.

Ben gripped Alice's arm. "We should leave now." He didn't mean to be curt, but these men pursuing her were persistent, and he didn't expect them to give up. As they became more desperate, they'd take more risks. One had already injured a police officer. Obviously, they'd been told to get Alice by any means possible. He and Alice needed to move, ASAP.

She took a quick breath and stared at him, eyes narrowed. She hesitated, and he wondered if he was going to have to waste precious time convincing her. Then she nodded and let him lead her to his SUV. She got in the passenger seat without another word. He looked at her again, assessing how she was responding. His job would be much more difficult if she fell apart.

She buckled up her seat belt and turned to him with a raised eyebrow. There was the teacher again. That was probably the exact look she gave students who were slow to respond to a question. She wasn't going to fall apart, and she didn't want to be pacified. Good.

He closed the passenger door, made his way around the vehicle and jumped in the driver's door, which he'd left open. He pulled it closed, buckled up his own belt and slammed the vehicle into gear, heading back the way he'd come.

He needed to get to Toronto, but he didn't want to follow the same route the attackers had taken. He had no intention of getting into a confrontation, not with Alice Benoit in the vehicle with him. It would be better to take a circuitous route. Something was very wrong, and everything indicated to there being a bad apple in what was supposed to be the good guys' basket.

Ben was sure there must be a mole in the police department feeding the gang information. Right now, he couldn't trust anyone. There might be just one mole in the department, but there were a lot of voices that could relay the information the mole needed.

Alice closed her eyes. She was praying and struggling to maintain her calm facade. Now that the initial adrenaline had abated, she was shaky, and part of her longed to give in to the fear. The tears were there, waiting to be released. But she couldn't. She didn't know why, but she was in danger. Real danger. She couldn't afford to fall apart, not if she was going to get out of this.

She'd known there was something off about the intruders in her house. They were no thieves. When the super had told the three of them to head to the detachment office, she'd known he had a reason. She'd accepted his suggestion and been willing to wait for answers, but the attack on the police car was far beyond anything she could have imagined.

Alice had been afraid for Henry many times, but she'd never found herself in that kind of danger. This kind of thing was totally unheard of in their small community, and she knew it was because of her. No way could this be a coincidence. She had an enemy, and she had no idea why or even what they looked like.

She looked over at her protector. Ben Parsons knew what was going on. These attacks hadn't confused him. There was a reason behind them, and he knew what it was.

Since Lychford was a small community and everyone knew everyone at some level, Alice knew some basic information about Ben. He'd come to Lychford from Toronto. He was about the same age as Henry, if Henry were still alive. He was single, or at least hadn't arrived with a partner. He was a career cop, and she expected he was as committed to his job as Henry had been. That made for an excellent police officer, but it wasn't always as desirable in a husband.

Henry had always maintained his appearance, but Ben was scruffy, pushing the boundaries of what the dress code allowed for police officers. He didn't look like someone you'd take to a fancy party, but he did look tough and able. Right now, Alice was happy with that.

She was quietly praying and marshaling her thoughts, waiting to get to the detachment so she could demand some answers, when Ben turned off the highway and onto a secondary road.

She turned to him, fear gripping her again.

"Aren't we going in to Lychford?" The detachment office meant safety, familiarity. It meant this would all be over.

He shook his head.

"Do you want to tell me what's going on here?" She struggled to keep her voice level. She expected to get some answers. Either that or she was going to get somewhere she felt safe. She reached into her bag to feel for her phone, her lifeline to the people she knew.

He glanced her way. Fear was seeping like cold into her body, but she met his gaze.

"We're not going to the detachment, because I don't think you're safe there."

Alice's jaw dropped. She knew almost every person working at the detachment office by name. She trusted every one of them.

Something was very, very wrong. Had it only been an hour ago that her life was ordinary?

"Why?" she asked. "Is it something connected to Henry?"

He tapped his fingers on the steering wheel and looked in the rearview mirror. Then he took another side road, and Alice tensed.

Ben let out a breath. "It's nothing to do with your husband."

She frowned. "You might not believe this, but those men who were in my house? They weren't looking for something to steal. They were looking for me. I heard them talking. The police car I was in was just run off the road and shot at. Do you think that's just a coincidence?" She heard her voice rising and fought for control.

He shook his head. "No, it's not a coincidence."

"Why do they want me?"

"It's because of your son."

Alice thought her stomach might have literally dropped about a foot. In fact, it was probably under her seat, no longer in her body. There was a hollow, painful hole where it had been. She felt nauseated and clutched the door handle. *Chris? Anything but Chris!*

"What about Chris? Is he okay? He's on an expedition—"

"No. He isn't."

Alice wanted to argue but held her tongue. She wasn't sure she could make an intelligible sentence. This wasn't making sense. She wondered if she'd made a mistake by getting in the vehicle with Ben.

Had Ben somehow lost it? Should she try to placate him? What could he know about Chris? Her son had left on his trip before Ben even arrived in Lychford.

Ben glanced at her, and then continued, "Six months ago, your son was walking home from a lab session late one night. He took a shortcut and witnessed a murder. He's been in short-term witness protection since then, not on a research vessel in the Antarctic."

Alice stared at Ben. He wasn't looking at her. He was focused on the road again, checking his mirrors, obviously worried that someone could still follow them.

She fought down the fear and thought about what he'd said. It was hard to keep her brain on one thought. Fears, recollections, speculations—they were all pouring through her mind.

She replayed his statement. He spoke with authority. She tested his words against what she knew for a fact versus what she only knew because it was what she'd been told. She couldn't refute what he'd said. Witness protection could explain everything just as well as an expedition. Maybe better. She'd thought Chris was fortunate to get a last-minute chance to go to the Antarctic. Maybe too fortunate.

It had been a good story, and she hadn't questioned it. Her fear reformed as anger. Anger felt better, stronger. Anger that she'd been lied to. Anger that her son had been in danger. She was also a cop's widow. She might not like what they'd done, but she understood why, so she took a breath and unclenched her fists.

"Okay, if that's true, it's been six months since Chris left. Why is someone coming after me now?"

She saw Ben's lips tighten. He answered her second question first. "I think there's a mole somewhere in the ranks. Someone leaked Chris's name and information, and in so doing exposed you."

The thought shocked her. You heard about bad cops, but she hadn't met any. Police officers weren't perfect. They were human, and they could make mistakes, but this was something different. Knowing what officers went through together, it would be a harsh betrayal if this were true.

"Who?" she asked. Not that she expected him to name anyone she knew, but she'd like to know that this person was contained.

"No idea. It's not me, and that's as far as I can promise. It's my job now to keep you safe."

THREE

Alice leaned back in her seat. She forced her lungs to breathe in and out.

She had a lot to consider. Chris was in witness protection. She could believe that of him. He was his father's son. He would want to do the right thing no matter the cost to himself. Henry would be proud.

And as a result, someone was hunting her down. That meant they knew about Chris and wanted to stop his testimony.

"You think they're trying to coerce Chris's testimony by using me. Why now? It's been six months."

"The trial is scheduled to begin February eighteenth. Tomorrow. Chris was shot this morning as he was leaving a safe house."

Alice heard a sound escape her lips.

Ben gave her a quick glance. "He's fine. Sorry, should have led with that. He was just grazed by the bullet, like Toby. Don't worry. He's better guarded than the prime minister now. But someone leaked his name and whereabouts. And someone leaked about you. I got a call telling me about your son just after the 911 call came in about the home invaders. That's why I drove out to your house."

Alice worked it through. An attack on Chris, followed by one on her so quickly, before word even got to the detachment here. Whomever Chris was testifying against, it was someone big with people to do his or her bidding. The hair on her neck stood up. She found herself chewing on her bottom lip again.

"So where are we going? What's your plan? I need to see Chris!" Her voice was rising, and this time she didn't care. She only had this man's word for it that Chris was safe.

"We're going to see your son first thing. He's insisting on making sure you're safe before he testifies."

That also sounded like Chris. "Where is he?"

"St. Mike's Hospital in Toronto. That's where we're headed."

"Is he okay where he is? Really okay?"

Ben nodded. "Right now, I'd say he's the safest person in the country."

"But you said there's a mole. How can you be sure?"

"I think there's a mole, but I could be wrong. If there is a mole, they're either in witness protection or homicide. The guys watching Chris now are part of ETF. They're trained to deal with terrorists. They were not involved with the case before Chris was shot, so the mole can't be in that department."

Alice had her hands clenched. She glanced at the passing scenery. "Then why aren't we on the highway? You seem a little lost."

Ben glanced at her again.

"If someone on the inside is leaking information,

the guys after you will know where we are headed, and they might try to intercept us on the highway first, before we get anywhere more crowded. I don't know if the guys who broke into your house are the same guys who attacked the squad car, so we could be dealing with two groups. I don't want to run into any of them. They are obviously highly motivated, and at the moment there's only me to protect you. I'm good, but I'm outnumbered."

Alice shuddered. And once she started, she couldn't stop. Reaction was setting in.

Someone had shot her son and tried twice to abduct her. They'd shot Toby, a young man she'd known for years. She'd been in a car crash and was now driving down back roads with someone she didn't really know. She felt dizzy. Lightheaded. The scenery was spinning around her.

Ben eased off the gas pedal and pulled the SUV into a dirt drive. He drove in far enough through the trees so that they couldn't be seen from the road, carefully turned the vehicle to face back the way they'd come, and put the SUV in Park. He turned to observe her.

"Do you need a moment? I know this has all been a lot."

A lot? Yes, it had been a lot. Alice wrapped her arms around herself and bent over, trying to stop the shivering. She looked out the window and realized she had no idea where she was. How did she know this man was telling the truth? Maybe Ben was part of all this, the mole he was talking about. Maybe she'd fallen right into his trap by blindly trusting him.

He reached out a hand, and she flinched.

"How can I trust you?" she managed to say through trembling lips.

He jerked back, watched her for a moment, then nodded his head at the dash.

"Open the glove box."

She paused, staring at him.

"Go ahead."

She reached out a trembling arm, and after three attempts, she managed to open the glove-box door. Inside, she found a gun.

"Take it."

She hesitated. "Is it loaded?"

"Do you know how to check?"

She nodded.

"Then go ahead. Just don't point it this way. Not unless you feel threatened."

Alice swallowed and grabbed the cold metal.

She didn't know that much about guns, but Henry had insisted she understand the basics. While he was alive, they'd always had guns in the house, and he'd wanted her to know how to handle them safely.

This gun was the same as the one Henry had been issued, a lightweight 9mm, and she was able to check that it was, in fact, loaded. The ritual helped to settle her nerves, and holding the weapon gave her some confidence.

"Are you a good shot?" Ben asked her.

Alice shook her head. She looked down at the weapon. Obviously, in the small interior of the SUV it wouldn't take a good shot to do fatal damage, but outside? She couldn't guarantee that she'd hit anything she aimed at.

"Alice—" He stopped. "Sorry, Mrs. Benoit—"

"I think you can call me Alice now," she said with a flash of a tremulous smile. If he had saved her, possibly from death, they didn't need to be formal. And if he was abducting her...

"Alice, the people after you are willing to shoot. I don't know if they missed anything vital on Toby by accident or on purpose, but I wouldn't assume they aren't willing to seriously harm or kill someone."

Alice thought that comment revealed a lot about whatever her son had become mixed up in. And it did not reassure her one bit.

"If you're not a good shot, I'd feel more comfortable if I was the one holding the gun in case we cross paths with them again. But I want you to feel safe. Are you up to driving?"

Alice frowned. He'd surprised her. He was risking a lot here. Henry had told her that she could only use his gun as a last resort if he'd been incapacitated. Ben was giving her a weapon, a loaded weapon. Was he playing her? Or was he on the level?

He answered her unspoken questions. "If you're driving, you can choose any route you want. That way you have control, but we do need to get away from these men looking for you. We should get to Toronto as soon as possible. I want to get you to your son, and then get you someplace safe until the trial is over. You need to decide quickly. If there's someone on the inside working for the bad guys, this vehicle might be easily traced."

Traced by the mole, who could relay it to the threatening men who'd attacked her and were probably not far away. He was right. They needed to move, and she had to decide. Now.

"Okay, I'll drive."

Ben got out and walked around the front of the vehicle. Alice undid her seat belt and scooted behind the wheel. The SUV was still running. She had the gun. She had the vehicle. She could leave Ben behind, that was if she didn't hit him with the SUV as she pulled out.

But the fact that he'd given her all the power convinced her he wasn't a threat to her. He'd had ample opportunity to abduct her, to hurt her, but he hadn't. Instead, he'd given her the opportunity to do harm to him.

Lord, I'm going to trust You sent this man to help me. Watch over us, and keep Your hand on Chris, and on Toby and Dale.

Ben climbed in, and Alice handed the gun over to him.

"Thanks." She saw his rigid posture relax. He knew just how vulnerable he'd made himself.

He checked the gun over for himself. Then he looked at her. "This should work. If the wrong people find us, I'm a pretty good shot. Are you good to drive all the way to the hospital?"

This wasn't a situation where Alice should blurt out the first conciliatory answer that came to mind. Honesty was her best option if she wanted to help Ben keep her safe. She didn't like to drive in Toronto. The traffic, the construction, the lack of parking... The transit system wasn't bad.

"When I go into Toronto, I normally drive to the

first subway station," she said. "I don't like driving in the city, so I take the subway or a bus."

"Perfect," Ben said. "I never take transit. Anyone trying to guess my movements won't expect that. We'll need a place to park the SUV when we get close."

Alice had one more question. She stared through the windshield, looking out at the scenery but not seeing the trees and snow around her. The cold she was feeling had nothing to do with the outside temperature.

"If things go wrong, if they get me, what will they do? Will they kill me?" She made an effort to keep her voice level. She didn't want to push Ben into empty reassurances, and she was afraid that she'd panic if he told her the truth, but she did need to know what she was dealing with.

Out of the corner of her eye, she saw Ben's gaze narrow on her. He was probably debating just what he could safely tell her. She did her best to present a calm demeanor, though her heart was pumping much like it had back in the hidey-hole less than an hour ago.

"I'm not going to freak out." She hoped not. Her faith was supposed to be strong enough for this. She'd find out.

Ben nodded. He'd made his decision.

"They won't want to kill or seriously harm you. They'll have no leverage with your son unless they have you alive."

That made sense. It also petrified her, to be called leverage. So what would they do to her if they got their hands on her, she wondered? Before she could ask, Ben continued.

"If they get you and think Chris still plans to testify, they'll hurt you, not fatally, and send him proof to put more pressure on him."

Alice swallowed. She really didn't want to test her faith in that situation. Maybe it made her a coward, but the thought of being in their hands scared her.

"If Chris does back down, would they release me?"

Ben looked at her gravely. "They could."

She felt goose bumps. From the way Ben said that, she got the feeling he didn't think they would let her go.

"You don't think they would, do you? What do you think they'd do?" She turned her head toward him. He leaned back against the seat, and she was sure he was going to sugarcoat it, but she didn't want that. She wanted to know.

"For real. I need to know how much trouble I'm facing. If I'm prepared, I'm less likely to make a stupid mistake."

He sighed. "Your son witnessed a murder. So that's not a line these people are afraid to cross. And they won't want to risk being identified and prosecuted for kidnapping. In my experience, someone in your position would never be seen again."

Alice looked back out the window. Logically, she could understand there were people out there that were that evil, that ungodly, but she'd always been in a safe bubble. She'd never been around people like that.

She sent up a quick prayer for strength. Her faith had never been tested like this, not when Henry had been hurt, not even when he'd had his heart attack and had been rushed to the hospital.

She'd have to trust that God had a plan. She hoped

that plan didn't involve her being led into the valley of death, but it was possible. Right now, it seemed that His plan had been to send this man beside her to protect her.

Lord, guide me. Guide us. Alice breathed as she put the vehicle in gear.

"I'd prefer not to be caught. So let's go."

Ben gave her a nod of approval.

"Should we keep to the back roads?"

Ben rubbed his chin as he considered her question. "I'm worried about time. I hope we've thrown off whoever was after you, but now we need to get some distance between us and the bad guys. I don't know how long we'll have until they start to look for this SUV, but we want to be done with it before that happens. The main road will be faster."

Alice checked for traffic and then turned right. If God had sent Ben her way, she'd take his advice.

FOUR

Ben relaxed slightly. For a moment, he'd wondered if this was when Alice would fall apart. It would be understandable, but it would also be problematic. So far, Alice was demonstrating a lot of strength.

He reconsidered his assumptions about the situation they were in. He tried not to jump to conclusions, but this was a case where he couldn't wait for all the evidence to be docketed. He didn't like the thought that someone on the inside was sharing information with a criminal, but until he could find a better explanation, he wasn't going to take a chance. Not with Alice's safety, not with her life on the line.

If he'd been on his own, he'd have driven straight to the hospital to meet with the team there to get more information. But as things were, if someone on the inside heard that the abductions had failed and that he had vanished with Alice, they'd start tracking his vehicle. And when they found his vehicle, they'd find Alice.

He thought they had time before that happened. Whoever he'd scared off after the car ramming had to report back. They would expect Ben and Alice to be on their way to the detachment in Lychford and would look for them along that route. It would take some time to realize Ben had gone AWOL and to then come after his vehicle. At least, that's how he hoped things would work out.

He looked in the side mirror next to him. The only vehicle he saw was a car far back that was slowly falling farther behind. It didn't look like they were being tracked, not yet anyway. Not by any car. There were other ways to track them.

He looked over at her. Beside her, resting on the seat at her hip was her purse.

"Do you have your phone?"

Alice nodded.

Ben pulled out his own phone and fiddled with it before returning it to his pocket.

"Where is it?"

"In my bag." She gasped as he reached for her purse. "What are you doing?" She tried to grab at it with her free hand.

"I need to turn your phone off. It could be traced."

She put her hand back on the wheel. "I'm just not accustomed to strangers helping themselves to my things," she said shortly.

"Sorry. I needed to get our phones turned off before we forget. I don't want anyone to be able to track you on this and our location get back to the wrong people. They might already be trying to trace it. We're getting close to the city limits."

He pulled out her phone and pressed the off button until the screen went blank.

"The mole." She drew in a breath. "Do you have any ideas who it is?"

He looked over at Alice. She was concentrating on the road and fortunately was a competent driver. Ben was always a little itchy when he was a passenger, but he'd felt compelled to give her a reason to trust him and to feel safe.

Alice glanced in the rearview mirror regularly. Her grip on the steering wheel was tight, knuckles white, and her forehead was creased.

He'd told her she was at risk of being tortured and killed, and she'd handled it well. He might as well share his fears about the mole.

"Your son is involved in a high-profile case. The way I see it, there are two probable scenarios. It could be someone new to the force, someone still boots-on-the-street level who just happened to get wind of what is going on with Chris and didn't realize what they'd revealed. If they only knew where you and Chris were, it's bad enough, but if that's the case, once we get the two of you somewhere safe, it's over. That's not as difficult to deal with as the alternative."

"And what's the alternative?"

"The alternative is that the mole is someone higher up, and that this case is important enough to risk his or her cover. And if so, there's a good chance it's someone I know."

Ben had worked in both homicide and witness protection, the departments that had been involved in the case up until now. Someone could have been doing a lot of damage from inside.

"You think it's the second option, don't you?"

Although her hands were still clenched tightly on the steering wheel, her voice was soft.

Did she understand how much that thought gutted him?

"I'm afraid it is."

It made him angry. Angry that someone would betray his or her fellow officers. Angry that he, Ben, had given everything to this job, and someone else would jeopardize that so easily. It would take a while to trace every officer who had information on Chris and to investigate each one. Alice didn't have that time.

Ben was going to get Alice safely delivered to the ETF unit, and then he wanted to be involved in the investigation into the mole. He wasn't sure why, but this felt personal. Someone had been willing to turn on his or her own. A bad cop hurt everyone. But now he had a job to do, and it was proving to be challenging.

He didn't want to call for assistance, because he wasn't sure what might get back to the mole. He was on his own. He had someone depending on him, a civilian, so he needed to get things right.

The fear of making a wrong decision, one that might result in someone being hurt or killed, had his fists balling in tension.

He had never imagined a scenario where he'd go AWOL without his cop family. But he was becoming more and more convinced that there was a mole on the inside. It was the only explanation for Chris Benoit getting shot. He'd never before tried to handle things on his own. He wasn't James Bond. He was just a regular cop, and cutting himself off from support made him deeply uncomfortable.

The other challenge was Alice herself.

She was an attractive woman, he thought again. More laugh lines than frown lines showed on her face, and her long dark hair was pulled back in a casual ponytail. She was comfortable in her skin.

She didn't panic in a tight spot, so she had courage. Smart, too. He hoped her husband had appreciated her.

No. There was no time for that kind of idiocy. He could not be interested in Alice. He just needed to get her safely to her son. Whether she was vain, brave, smart or pretty shouldn't factor in. He couldn't afford any distractions.

Distractions were often fatal, as he'd learned the hard way.

Alice was tense during the drive, eyeing every passing vehicle, looking for the one she'd seen briefly before it rammed the police car. Her thoughts were scattered as she worried about what had happened to Chris and tried to figure out what was happening with the mole Ben believed might be deep in the police department. She wondered if the police had locked up her house, how Chris had gotten into this, how she was going to replace all her ID and…

No ID, no wallet, no money. If they weren't driving directly to the hospital, how was she going to get there without any cash or her credit card? At home, they knew her at the bank, but in Toronto…

She glanced over at her companion.

"Um, Mr. Parsons…"

He turned concerned brown eyes to her. "Ben is fine. Is there a problem?"

"Just a little one. I hope. I don't have any money. Actually, I don't have a wallet at all. Whoever broke into my place took that."

She watched the road but slanted a glance at him to check his reaction. His heavy frown wasn't reassuring.

"What did you have in the wallet?"

She mentally tallied the normal contents. "A bit of cash. Credit and debit cards. All my identification, including my driver's license."

She glanced at her hands on the wheel. "Maybe I shouldn't be driving."

He snorted. "I think that's the least of our problems right now. Anything else?"

"Health card, pictures, including one of Chris, if that's an issue. In-case-of-emergency contact information, a few receipts..."

Her voice trailed off as she tried to remember if there was anything else of note.

"I'll keep that in mind," he answered. "But I don't think you'll need any of that to get in to see your son. Not when you're with me, if that's what you're worried about."

"No," she agreed. "But I have no money to pay for traveling in the city and no way to get any."

She could see him frowning from the corner of her gaze.

"I can take care of that."

"I don't like being in your debt. Besides, if we were to get split up—"

His frown deepened.

"You have a point about the money. If things go well, it's a non-issue. But if not... Here's what I suggest. We'll stop at a bank machine, and I'll pull out all the cash I can. I'll loan you enough to keep you going, just in case."

Just in case. In case things went badly.

Alice considered his offer. It was difficult to put her faith in someone she'd just met, but she did put her faith in God, and He had provided Ben.

"Thank you." She hoped she'd be able to return the money to him once she saw Chris at the hospital.

There were more cars on the road now, and she had vehicles ahead and behind her. More cars and more people gave her more things to worry about, but it might also make her safer, since any attempt to abduct her would attract attention. She also hoped they could get lost in amongst the other vehicles. Of course, this all might make the men after her more desperate.

They passed a big-box store with a large parking lot.

"Pull in here," Ben said, watching the vehicles around them. "Around back."

Alice followed his instructions and parked the marked SUV behind the store. No one followed them.

"I saw a sign for a bank down half a block. We can leave the vehicle here, out of sight, get some cash at the bank machine, then catch a bus to the subway."

Alice nodded.

"We could be traced to here, if they track the SUV," he said. "And they could possibly track us to the bank with the cameras from the ATM, but from there on, we have a good chance of being lost."

Alice had a hard time believing this was real. She wasn't dreaming, was she? She took a quick look in the mirror and was shocked at what she saw.

She grabbed her purse and pulled out her hairbrush. The home invaders hadn't been interested in that. She quickly released her hair clip and teased out the knots that had accumulated while she'd been hiding in the closet and then knocked into the ditch. Pulling her hair back smoothly into the clip, she then brushed down her clothes that had picked up a lot of dust from the closet and some other things she didn't want to identify.

Ben regarded her with amusement, and she frowned at him. "What?"

He shook his head. "Are you worried about the fashion police?"

"I don't want to be noticed, do I? People will remember me if I look like I've just been dragged through a bush," Alice defended her actions.

Ben nodded. But as she checked herself out again in the mirror, he asked, "Do I need your brush?"

Alice knew he was teasing her. He probably hoped that would help her relax. She wasn't terrifically vain, but she felt better if she looked her best. It might be silly, but it gave her more confidence. Something she didn't have much of right now.

Well, what was sauce for the goose…

She smiled sweetly and passed over the brush.

Ben looked at it for a moment, then he surprised her by adjusting the mirror and quickly swiping at his hair. He passed it back just as politely.

Okay, she was scared, worried and completely out of her comfort zone, but she did appreciate a sense of humor. It had been a trying, terrifying day so far, but she could feel tension easing out of her shoulders with this joke, and it made her trust him even more.

FIVE

Ben was surprised by her gesture with the brush. He was more and more impressed by Alice. He had no doubt she was frightened, but she'd kept her sense of humor.

He'd like to think she'd wanted to look good for him, but he had to brush that thought away. There were other things to concentrate on now. Like getting Alice to the hospital safely.

"If we're going to take the subway to St. Mike's, how long do you think it should take us?" he asked, distracting himself.

Alice bit her lip again as she looked around and did some calculations in her head. "About an hour, an hour and a half if there are crowds or something holds us up. Of course, it's possible that they have to shut something down, in which case it would take most of the day."

She confirmed his own calculations. This was another reason he didn't like being dependent on transit. But now that they were within the city limits, leaving his conspicuous vehicle behind, they didn't have to rush.

They were far away from Alice's home and the places she normally would be. No one could trace them right now. The priority was to stay safe and get to the hospital sometime today. He wanted to be sure the mole didn't know when that would be.

"That's what I thought. I'm going to send in a message. I'll let the ETF team know you're okay, and we'll be at the hospital in four hours."

She tilted her head. "Providing a buffer so they don't get worried if we're held up?"

Ben shook his head. "I've checked the transit reports. There's nothing to hold us up right now. But if the mole hears this, I want him to tell whoever is hunting for you that you'll be arriving well after you're already there and safe. If they set up a trap, I don't want to walk into it. If transit becomes a problem and we get held up somewhere along the line, then we'll catch a cab."

Her eyes widened, and she swallowed, but she nodded.

He relayed the message and then shut down everything on the vehicle that could give away its location.

"Ready?" he asked.

"Yes. I need to see Chris." He could see the determination on her face.

They opened the SUV doors and slid out. Ben led the way around the building, trying to watch every corner while looking inconspicuous.

No one was paying any attention to them. They walked out into the light midday crowds, and no one seemed to care as they made their way over to the bank.

They had to wait in line while people in front of

them used the banking machines. Ben searched for the cameras and did his best to keep their faces out of the direct line of sight. The cameras meant that he and Alice could eventually be traced to this location, if the search got that detailed, but he thought it would take a while.

That was only in the worst-case scenario, anyway.

Once the mole realized Ben and Alice weren't going to the detachment, he might be able to discover Ben's message and hear they were going to the hospital, but he'd expect them later.

When the woman in front of him finished with the bank machine, he took his turn, face away from the cameras, and requested the daily maximum in cash.

If it had been his bank, the branch he was familiar with, he'd have risked going inside and getting more money, just in case. But it wasn't his bank, and he didn't want to take the time to detour here. After all, he expected they'd be safe in about an hour. The subway didn't cost that much.

He kept a hundred dollars for himself and passed the rest to Alice. She started to shake her head, and he placed his hand around hers, the one holding the money, and lightly squeezed.

She stiffened for a moment, and then put the money in her purse, no questions. They left the machine for the next person in line and headed out.

They turned west, in the direction of the bus stop.

"That's a lot of money," she said. "What if you need some?"

"I'm not the one being hunted. If I'm separated from you, I can call a friend."

She blinked as she took that in. He hated upsetting her, but she needed to be aware and prepared. She'd asked for the truth back there, and he had decided to give her that. He wasn't going to sugarcoat things now.

"Chris is at St. Mike's, and he's as safe there as he can be. Get there yourself, and you'll be taken care of."

"Couldn't I just go to a police station?" she asked out of the corner of her mouth.

"If you go into a station, there's a protocol they'll follow. The mole might be in that chain of information, and you'll be at risk again."

"Do you really think he would get that information??"

He took a moment to look over at her. She was staring ahead, watching where they were going, but her jaw was set. She wasn't going to fall apart.

"I'm afraid so."

"Okay." She turned and smiled at him a little shakily. "Let's not get split up, though. I'm nervous carrying this much of your money."

He felt a rush of warmth and smiled back. "Let's not." This was becoming more than a job. He didn't want anyone hurting this woman.

It was good that he would hand her over soon. Any kind of distraction compromised his ability to do what he needed to do.

"There's a bus stop ahead. Should we wait for the bus?"

"Are you cold?"

She shook her head. "Not while we're moving."

"It's only a few more stops to the subway. I think it's just as smart to walk."

She nodded and kept walking. She didn't ask any further questions, but he could see the tension in her body. He hoped it would be over soon.

In fifteen minutes, they entered the subway station. Ben noted the cameras again as he led the way to the ticket window and purchased two one-day passes. He had considered paying just enough for this trip, but in the end, he decided the day passes were best.

Just in case.

Alice raised her eyebrows but didn't say anything. He passed one to her. Alice followed as he pushed his way through the barricades and headed down the stairs to the platform. He scanned the platform, looking for any familiar faces or anyone who paid them more attention than expected.

The problem was he didn't know who to watch for.

There wasn't a large crowd on the subway platform at this time of day. Alice checked the display monitor overhead for the expected arrival of the next subway car and was surprised to find it was already lunchtime. Her stomach tightened, reminding her that breakfast had been a long time ago. She could wait to eat. She wanted to see that Chris was safe, and she wanted to feel safe herself.

She trusted Ben, and so far she hadn't found any reason to regret that. She did feel safe with him. Maybe it was his size, or his calm competence, but having him here felt like having a safety net. He made her feel safe, even though he kept reminding her she wasn't.

She didn't know if Ben was a believer. Her instincts told her he was taking this responsibility solely on himself, as though the burden was all on his shoulders. She'd like to let him know that ultimately her trust was in God, but then the subway train pulled in, and they got on.

Ben placed his hand on her back, keeping them connected. The crowds were minimal, but they didn't want to be separated. She felt protected, cared for. In many ways, Ben reminded her of Henry. He was a good officer, obviously, and he was willing to risk himself for her.

But being a good police officer meant that the job always came first. Alice understood that, but there had been times with Henry that she had wanted to come first. She hadn't planned on dating anyone after Henry died, but if she did, it would be someone who would put her ahead of everything else, even his job. Otherwise, what was the point?

She shook her head. Why was she thinking like this? There was nothing going on here to make her think about dating again. Ben was doing his job. That's all. She needed to get a grip. She'd only met the man a couple of hours ago.

The subway train they were on was one of the new ones. Instead of a chain of separated cars, the cars were open from first to last, and that meant they could walk all the way through the train if they wished. Ben led the way to a central car, and they sat down. He sat back, as if relaxed, but his gaze was constantly moving, watching everyone else in their area, pinning down anyone walking through their car.

Alice watched the dots marking the stops on the subway map light up as they reached each station. She counted down to where they would get off for the hospital. Eight. Five. Four, three, two...

The doors opened, and Alice felt Ben tensing up beside her. She looked around, wondering what he'd seen to affect him this way. Suddenly, he grabbed her hand and pulled her out of the doors with him just before they closed.

Alice balanced on her toes, looking for where the threat was coming from, but Ben had relaxed. She turned to him and frowned.

"What happened?"

"Nothing," he said, smiling.

"Then what was that about? I thought... I thought..." Alice heard her voice quavering.

Ben's smiled faded. He put a hand to her cheek. "Sorry, I didn't mean to scare you. I thought we'd hop off here and walk the last bit. I just checked to see if anyone was coming after us. No one looked at us or tried to follow us off, so that's all good."

Alice drew back and took a breath. "You're right, that's good. I guess I'm just a little stressed."

"It's a stressful situation. I don't mean to upset you. I'm concentrating on getting you to the hospital safely, whatever it takes."

He looked at her with a level gaze, checking how she was doing. She nodded. He was being a good cop. Exactly what he was supposed to be. There was no reason for her to be disappointed by that. Or for her cheek to feel the warmth of his touch after his hand was gone.

They walked the last three blocks to the hospital without incident. It was cold enough for Alice to see her breath, but the crowds of people rushing by ignored them. Everyone had their own place to be, and they had no time or inclination to check out the others passing by. Except for Ben. His gaze was always in motion, watching the noon commuters.

Once they arrived at St. Mike's, Ben led them through a side door, and, again, no one paid them any attention. Everyone was rushing by with purpose, and Alice wasn't part of that. It was a relief. She could feel the tension seeping out of her body.

As concern for her own safety abated, Alice found her worries about Chris increasing. For the last couple of hours, she'd been on a toboggan run down a bumpy hill, concentrating almost exclusively on her own survival. Wham, someone was in her house and she had to hide. Bump, the car was in the ditch, there were gunshots and she had to flee. Now that she had arrived safely at her destination, she had time to think about her son.

She no longer had room to think about anything else.

Chis hadn't been on an expedition. He'd lied to her. He'd been in danger, and he'd been hurt. She was nervous, angry and relieved.

Ben didn't check in at a desk. Alice wasn't sure if that was to maintain their cover, or just because he was familiar with the hospital. She was so anxious to see her son that she didn't care. Ben led her to the elevators and pushed the up button. The elevator car that stopped was empty, and they rode up in silence.

She knew when they'd gotten to the correct room. There was a uniformed guard outside the door, and she and Ben were under surveillance from the moment they exited the elevator. It was a comfort to think that Chris was this well protected.

Once they'd been identified, Ben stood back so she could go into the room first.

There were four men in uniform inside the room, but she didn't pay attention to them. Her gaze was focused on the man in jeans on the bed, his arm in a sling.

He was a total stranger.

Not Chris. It was a trap.

SIX

Every muscle in her body tightened. She turned, ready to flee the room, looking for hands trying to stop her. Where was Ben? How had he let this happen?

Then she noticed the mischievous look on the face of one of the uniformed men. A very familiar face.

"Chris?"

All the tension and adrenaline vanished, leaving her almost faint.

"Mom." He came from the back wall to gather her in a warm hug. "I've missed you."

Alice reined in the anger that followed her fear. "I'm sure it was lonely in the *Antarctic*."

Chris released her. "Sorry, Mom. I didn't have a choice about that. We needed a good cover, and it had to be something pretty serious for me to leave you alone over Christmas. Were you okay?"

Relief now won out over every other emotion. Alice patted his cheek. "I was fine. How were you?"

Chris shrugged. "I was able to keep up with classes remotely. It was a little boring. But…"

Alice understood. Chris would always do the right thing.

"I thought you were hurt. How come you're not the one on the bed?"

"I was just grazed, honestly. But considering everything that happened, Dan here is going to be a decoy."

Alice looked at the young man risking himself to protect her son. She smiled her thanks. Chris wasn't the only one doing his duty.

Alice felt her throat close up. He was an adult now, but she couldn't completely separate this young man in a borrowed uniform from the baby, toddler, child and adolescent she'd watched over the years. Chris narrowed his glance at her.

"You're okay, right? I didn't want anyone to freak you out. You knew I was fine?"

Alice drew in a long breath. "As fine as I could be after hearing my kid had been *just grazed* by a bullet. But you're safe now?"

Chris shrugged. "Should be. I've got a new group of protectors, and they're not very happy about what happened this morning."

Alice looked at one of the men in the room. His lips were pressed tightly together, and when he caught her gaze, he nodded. He looked capable enough. And he was well armed.

"And you're really okay, Mom?" Chris asked. "I insisted I had to see you and make sure you're safe."

"I'm fine. I hid in the hidey-hole when the men broke in—"

"What?" Chris exploded.

Alice looked around, but none of the men met her gaze.

"They didn't tell you about the break-in? And the accident?"

Chris's eyes blazed, and he looked angrily at the other men. "No, no one told me anything."

Alice reached out and gripped his arm. "I'm fine. Some men broke into the house, so I hid in your dad's hidey-hole. They were scared off by the police arriving. Then, when we were on our way into the detachment, an SUV ran us off the road." She saw Chris was opening his mouth to yell, so she kept on. "Toby and Dale—you know them—they did an excellent job protecting me. The new superintendent scared the guys in the SUV away, and then he brought me here. I don't even have a graze on me."

Alice looked back and realized Ben still wasn't there. "Maybe he had to go—"

Ben reappeared in the doorway, and the relief that he was still watching out for her unwound the tension that had tightened her posture when she didn't see him. He'd become her safety blanket on this chaotic day.

"Ben?" She questioned his absence with just one word.

"I was just calling in. There's a team coming to keep you safe until your son has finished testifying."

Ben moved toward the two of them and held out a hand. "I assume you're Chris."

Chris paused a moment and then shook the proffered hand. "Thank you for taking care of my mother."

"Happy to. I appreciate what the two of you are risking."

Chris smiled. "My dad wouldn't have it any other way."

One of the men in the room, presumably the leader of the team, interrupted them. "We should move Mrs. Benoit as soon as possible, before anyone knows she's here."

Alice didn't want to let Chris go. She'd just seen him for the first time in months, and there was a lot to talk about. She clutched his arm. He smiled at her and put his good arm around her. He was taller than she was, and after years of looking up to her, she now looked up to him.

"The sooner this is over, the sooner we can get back to normal, Mom. I'm safe here, and they'll put you somewhere so that I know you're good. I'll be fine. We can catch up after."

"This is just temporary?"

He nodded. "I might not even have to testify. There's been talk of the guy getting immunity for testifying about the gang, so if that goes through, I'm free and clear. Then we'll have time for everything."

He emphasized the word *everything*.

"I will see you again, in either case, right?"

She didn't know what they'd do if for some reason he had to go into long-term witness protection, but she wanted to be involved.

She'd insist on it.

Chris shot a glance at the team around him. "Absolutely. You take care."

"If anything were to happen to you—" she started.

A look of determination crossed Chris's face. "Or you. When you're safe, let me know."

He looked around the room. "I need to know about anything that happens to my mother, and I need to know she's safe before I go into a courtroom." He turned back to Alice. "You call me, okay?"

Alice frowned. "I'm not supposed to use my phone."

"Whoever's guarding you will know how to get in touch with me."

Alice lowered her voice. "If there is a mole, it might go through the wrong person. How will I know you're really okay?"

Chris cocked his head. "Should we have a code? Pumpernickel?"

Alice glared at him. "I'm serious. We need something. I thought I could mention a present we got you, and you can respond with when you got it—birthday, or Christmas, or whatever."

Chris patted her shoulder. "Good one, Mom." He looked around the room. "I'm going to need to hear about a present my parents gave me before I go into court, okay?"

The same man nodded. Alice assumed he was senior to the others.

"Feel better?"

She squeezed his arm before letting it go. "Yes. And when this is over, we've got a *lot* to talk about."

He grinned at her, Henry's grin.

"Yeah, you can tell me off after this is all done. I love you, Mom."

"I love you, too, Chris. I'm praying for you." She hesitated, not wanting to leave, but everyone, the guards and Chris, all seemed to be waiting, ready to get on to the next thing once she was gone. She waved and walked into the hallway. She didn't want to leave Chris, but she'd learned this lesson with Henry. The Benoit men didn't like to be fussed over.

Alice turned to Ben, who had followed her out. "So what's the plan?"

"There's a team of trustworthy guys coming to take you to a safe house. I know the sergeant. I wouldn't pass you over to anyone I couldn't trust."

"I wish I were staying here," she said wistfully. The hospital felt so safe, so calm after her morning.

Ben shook his head. "The hospital has rules. We don't know how long the trial will be. We can't tie up space here, and we don't want to stay in a spot you're known to have been.

"You need to be stashed somewhere secure for the duration, and your son will be going back and forth to the courthouse. You'll be safer on your own once they get you stored away. I'll take you down to them when you're ready."

He sounded impatient, eager to have this over with. Alice nodded. She knew this was the right thing to do. Logically, it made sense. But on a baser level than logic, she didn't want to leave Ben. She felt safe with him.

She needed to remember she was a job to him. That's all.

And also that her ultimate trust was in God.

They returned to the elevators, and Ben pushed the down button. The doors slid open and they saw the car was half-full. Ben shook his head and let the doors close. He pushed the down button again, and this time, it opened on empty car. Ben used his hand on her back again to gently usher her inside. He selected the button for the lobby, and the doors slid closed.

"This should only be for a week or two, and then you'll get to go home again," he reassured her.

Alice nodded.

"I'd like to hear how things went, once you're back," he said.

Alice paused.

Was she reading too much into that? He wasn't asking her for a date, was he?

Alice hadn't really thought much about dating again. After twenty-five years of marriage, she still felt married most of the time. She wasn't, though. Maybe it was time to think about that.

Not now, when she had people chasing her. Soon, maybe? She had to admit she had noticed Ben in a way she hadn't noticed a man in a long time. But Ben was a cop. Alice had been there and done that. She'd paced the floor, canceled plans and spent too much time alone. She didn't have an unlimited future. She'd made the decision that she wasn't taking second place anymore. Solitary independence was better than that.

"Chris and I would be happy to let you know how it all turns out," she said to make sure she understood the limits of their relationship as well as him.

The elevator settled on the lobby floor, and Alice turned to the opening doors in relief. She found herself in the middle of the lobby, aware that she wasn't sure where to go or whom she was meeting.

Before she could panic, Ben was beside her, introducing her to a tall competent-looking man. Then Ben stepped back, and she followed her new protector and his silent partner out the swinging doors, mind still in a daze.

She heard yelling and the harsh screech of car brakes applied at the last minute. She tried to move, but the car hit her just hard enough to throw her off balance, and she fell.

Her arm was yanked, and she looked up to see a stranger's cold eyes focused on her, a gun in his hand.

She was caught.

SEVEN

While Ben considered his next move, Alice and her protectors carefully made their way through the revolving doors at the front of the hospital. There was a car waiting for them outside of those doors.

Suddenly, another vehicle rocketed to the entrance, knocking down Alice and the two officers with her. As soon as Ben realized what was going on, he was in motion. He raced through the doors, responding before anyone else had started to move.

A man jumped out of the attacking vehicle. He had a gun in one hand and grabbed Alice's arm with the other, pulling her up roughly from the ground, his weapon aimed at the team protecting her.

The officers in charge had taken the brunt of the impact from the vehicle and couldn't respond in time, even if the perp had been unarmed. Ben hadn't tried a flying tackle since he played football in high school, but he launched himself at the man dragging Alice to the waiting vehicle.

Ben kept himself in shape. He was a big guy but his body was solid muscle, and he landed hard on the man's back. The man stumbled, and instinctively broke the fall with his hands, leaving Alice free as he tumbled down. Alice scrambled away as soon as his grip loosened.

Smart woman.

The rest of Alice's team were now out of their vehicle. The fallen attacker regained his feet and barely made it into the car as Ben, back on his feet, tried to catch hold of him. The driver reversed, knocking down at least two pedestrians before shifting into Drive and squealing away.

Alice fled. The protection team was distracted with two members down and one officer trying to relay the details of the attackers' vehicle on the radio. There were also two injured civilians and spectators crowding around.

"I'll get her," Ben said.

The officer shook his head. "She's ours now."

Ben indicated the chaos around them with one hand. "She's gone. She doesn't know you. I might be the only one she trusts now."

The man knew Ben. They went way back. That was the reason Ben had been willing to pass Alice over to them. He hesitated, then took another glance around before nodding reluctantly. Ben ignored a sore hip and started to run in the direction he'd last seen Alice.

Alice had made good use of her time. She was no longer in sight. Ben halted his run, heart pounding loud in his chest from shock and exertion. He forced himself to think rather than react.

She'd want to find cover. She didn't know whom to trust, so she wouldn't go where people were. She'd initially headed in this direction, but she'd want to find some protection as soon as possible. She wasn't used to Toronto, didn't know it inside and out like he did.

He should be able to figure this out. He looked for physical structures to hide behind.

He wasn't sure if Alice would trust even him now. As soon as he'd passed her over to a supposedly safe team, she'd been attacked again. She'd been attacked three times in one day, and she'd managed to escape three times. He was afraid her luck would eventually run out.

He walked the streets surrounding the hospital, following a grid pattern, ignoring the crowds on the sidewalk. He paused to call her name quietly whenever he thought there was a place she might have gone to ground, waiting for a lull in the people passing by so as not to attract attention. Half a block away, he finally heard her voice from behind a dumpster.

He didn't realize how worried he was until the relief of hearing her voice swept over him. She was alive, she still trusted him and he had another chance to keep her safe.

Ben didn't look her way. He paused and leaned against a wall casually, taking out his phone as if he were checking for messages, while in reality he turned the phone off. They were going to need to go off-grid again.

He scanned the area for any indication of danger. Not seeing anything obvious, he spoke. "Are you okay?"

"I think so. No bones broken, and no bullet wounds." Her voice wobbled a bit as she repeated her earlier response. "What happened there?"

His jaw clenched. "The mole struck again. They knew you were leaving the hospital."

He waited while she processed that.

"Are those officers okay?"

His mouth curved into a half smile. Even in the midst of her own problems, she was worrying about other people. There was a lot to like about Alice Benoit.

"I think so, but I didn't stick around to find out. Fortunately, they're outside a hospital, so they'll get care right away."

"What are we going to do now?" Her voice quavered again, but he warmed to know she was trusting him to help her. She'd said *we*.

"I don't know who I can trust now. I think it's just you and me." It was stupid, but in spite of everything, he felt a trickle of happiness that he was going to be with her for a while yet.

He made himself fight that feeling. If he didn't want any more close calls, any more problems, he was going to have to be objective. He was going to have to be better than he'd been on any job before, because now he was working solo. He couldn't do that if he was distracted.

As he well knew, emotions were distracting. Fatally so.

"Okay," Alice answered.

He pressed a few buttons on the dead phone, pretending he was looking up something for the benefit of anyone watching them. A quick glance around suggested no one was paying attention, but he wouldn't take any chances. Not with Alice.

"It's cold, and it's going to get colder. We can't leave you hiding back there, and it may take me some time to find a safe place to hole up."

"So what are you suggesting?" Her voice was getting stronger. Did she have that much faith in him?

"I think there's an advantage right now in being in a crowd where we're less likely to stand out."

"Really?"

He could hear the doubt in her voice.

"It's a bit of a risk. We don't know whom we need to avoid, and they must have some information on what we look like. But it's harder to pick someone out in a crowd, and riskier to attempt an abduction that way. The forecast is for freezing temperatures tonight. You can't stay put, so there's going to be a risk whatever we do."

"Back to the hospital, then?"

Ben shook his head.

"They'll probably be watching the hospital. They know you were there and might expect you to double back. It will be the starting point for any searches."

"What about Chris? "

"They were taking him out the back while you were leaving by the front door. You provided good cover for him."

"What's the plan, then?"

Ben rubbed his jaw. "I want to do something they won't expect. Something that isn't in the playbook they'll be using." He paused. "We're only a block away from the Eaton Centre."

The Eaton Centre was a large indoor mall in the heart of downtown Toronto. It stretched for blocks, was connected to an underground walkway and had subway stops attached to it. There were a lot of places for them to get lost. Lots of escape routes.

He hoped the people searching for them wouldn't have the same idea. But right now, there was no guaranteed safe spot. He waited to get Alice's response.

"How do we get there?" she eventually asked.

They had to go on foot. They were too close for a bus, and no taxi would want a one-block fare. Waiting for either would leave them exposed this close to the hospital. People would undoubtedly be looking for them. Unless…

Ben had an idea, but he wasn't sure how much she'd like it.

"They're looking for you right now. They may or may not expect me to be with you. We need to look as unlike what they're expecting as we can."

"Why do I think you're going to suggest something I won't like?"

Ben shrugged.

Alice sighed. "Okay, hit me."

Two minutes later, a couple strolled along the sidewalk toward Eaton Centre. He had his arm wrapped around her shoulder and she had hers around his waist. Their heads were close together, as if they were moments away from a kiss. Two lovers, lost in each other, ignoring everyone around them.

Ben tucked her as close to him as he could. It would foster the impression that they were a couple, and he felt better with her this near, leaving no space for someone to get to her without going through him. He liked the feel of her wrapped in his embrace. Even though she had a slight whiff of eau de garbage rising from her jacket, and even though she probably didn't want to see him after this adventure they were in, he liked this togetherness, this lack of being on his own. It had been a long time since he'd been close to someone, and he'd forgotten how good that contact could be.

They fit together well, walking as if they'd done this

countless times before. He could feel the trembling in her limbs as she tried to pretend this was normal, but she was tense. She'd been through a lot already, and he wasn't sure how much she could take. He needed to find them a safe place before it became too much for her.

He couldn't go to his place here in the city. He'd leased out his house when he started the assignment in Lychford, and once the department worked out that he was with Alice, as they undoubtedly would, any of his usual hangouts would be checked. He didn't want to call on any of his buddies, since a wrong word in any-one's ear could expose Alice again. He also didn't want to put his friends at risk.

Alice wouldn't be in immediate mortal danger if the bad guys got her. They needed to hold that threat over her son until he refused to testify. But after that... After that, who knew?

He wasn't going to share those fears with Alice again now. He needed her to be strong. He'd scared her enough, and what he hadn't done, the men chasing her had.

They were almost at the mall now. There was a big clothing store on the outside corner of the mall, providing an additional entrance. If they got in there undetected—

Someone shoved Ben to the ground. He twisted as he landed and saw a man with his arms around Alice. There was a car idling at the side of the road, driver at the ready.

They were trying to take Alice again.

EIGHT

Ben swung his leg around hard and connected with the abductor's calf, pushing through for all he was worth. The man stumbled and loosened his grip on Alice.

"Run!" Ben yelled at her, bringing his other foot around to try again.

The man was ready this time and jumped away. But Ben had distracted him sufficiently that Alice was able to wrench free and run to the door of the store.

Ben knew the man would follow her, so he rolled into the guy's feet. The man was able to get in a sharp kick to Ben's ribs, but as Ben kept rolling, he finally went down. He landed on Ben, who quickly flipped their positions and straddled the man's waist to keep him from following Alice.

He saw movement from the corner of his eye. Leaning his hands on the man under him, Ben saw the driver exit his car and run to the door of the store.

A crowd was now gathering around Ben and the man struggling beneath him. Ben could ask them to call for the police, but if the driver got Alice, it would be pointless. The man he'd captured might not even know where they were planning to take Alice, and even if he did know, once the gang knew the man had been captured, they'd change their plans.

Ben had a fraction of a second to decide, and he decided on Alice. He didn't ask anyone in the crowd to call 911, because he couldn't wait for backup to arrive. He stood and ran for the store, leaving the man on the ground.

At the doorway, he paused. A glance back showed the man he'd tackled was limping to the car, probably to request reinforcements. A glance inside the store showed no sign of Alice or anyone who looked like the driver he'd seen going after her.

Ben slowed his breathing and pushed into the store. Near the doorway to the mall, he saw someone in a jacket that looked like the one the driver had been wearing. He was heading into the mall.

Ben wasn't sure if the driver had noticed his face before the abduction attempt, but the man might remember Ben's clothing. With one eye on the man, who'd paused to look both ways in the mall, Ben stood behind a display rack, slid his jacket off, and stuffed it under some jeans. Moving around the store, he picked up a hat and shoved it on his head. Carefully keeping his profile toward the mall door, Ben slowly wandered in that direction, stopping to pick up a sweater and a shirt on the way. He was just a shopper looking for clothes.

He'd made his way close to the entrance, close enough to overhear the man on the phone.

"I'll watch this entrance to the mall—get the other doors covered. Once she's cornered, we can track her down."

Ben turned and kneeled down to pretend to tie his shoelace as the man swept his gaze over the store and then headed back to where he'd entered.

Ben stood and pretended to be interested in a selection of pants on the table in front of him while the man left. Ben retraced his own path until he was beside the door to the street, standing back enough to be invisible to anyone outside.

The two men from the car were talking. The man Ben had fought was gesturing at the other, and then he moved toward the large public doorway to the general part of the mall with a frown on his face. The other leaned on the car, watching the doorway Ben and Alice had gone through.

They had reinforcements on the way, so Ben and Alice had a window of time to get themselves somewhere else. He just needed to find Alice.

It was a big mall, and he had no idea where she was.

Alice stood in front of the changing room mirror, looking at but not seeing her own reflection. Instead, images of the day flashed through her vision, and she sank onto the bench provided for customers.

She had never prayed so much in one day, and her prayers were almost a nonstop stream of, *Help me! Help me! Help me!*

She thought of the two Lychford officers, Toby and Dale, one shot and one injured in the car accident. And the officers outside the hospital who had been hit by that car. She sent a quick prayer for their recovery and safety.

And Chris with the "just a graze" on his arm from a bullet. The prayer for her son's safety was more fervent, but she knew God would understand. She worried less about her own physical safety and more about how difficult it would be for Chris if he were faced with a choice between testifying or protecting her. She didn't want to put him in that situation, so she had to stay safe for another day or so.

How many days would he need to testify?

After the chaos at the hospital, she'd hidden behind the dumpster and prayed for wisdom and safety. Hearing Ben call her name had sounded like an answer to her prayers in an immediate and practical way.

After she'd turned down his invitation to meet up after this was all over, she hadn't expected to see him again, much less have him offer protection and risk himself for her. But again, when she was in need, he was there.

He was a good cop. One of the finest. And that was exactly why she didn't want to spend time with him, be attracted to him, get ideas about him. She'd been married to a good cop. There was a price that came with it. She'd paid for twenty-five years, and she didn't have it in her to pay it again.

Someone in the next changing room thumped the wall and giggled. It brought Alice back to her surroundings.

She couldn't stay in here for the next twenty-four hours. She needed to find Ben. She knew he'd be looking for her, and she didn't have the knowledge and connections to keep herself safe on her own.

If it were summer, or if they were back in Lychford, maybe, but they were in Toronto during a cold snap.

She sent up another prayer, asking God to keep Ben

safe and show her the way she needed to go. Then she stood, ready to deploy the resources she had on hand.

She grabbed the clothes she'd brought in. She'd done some thinking about this. If she had something new to wear and could look different, that should help keep her from being found easily. She also had the smell of the dumpster clinging to her clothes and wanted that gone. She'd buy these with the money Ben had given her and change in a bathroom in the mall. She'd have to repay him later. The clothes were just the latest item on a long list.

She left the change room with her choice of clothes, and looked around for the man who'd tried to abduct her or the driver who'd followed her into the store. There was no sign of them. With that worry gone, she looked for Ben. The store wasn't crowded in the middle of the day on a weekday, so she was soon able to locate him, even with a strange hat he had on. He had a way of moving that she already recognized. He was headed back to the outside exit, gaze forward. She followed that gaze and saw the man who'd chased her heading out.

Her breath caught, and she quickly turned away, looking down at a display of skinny jeans she wouldn't dare try to wear. She fought down the fear, reminding herself that she had Ben, and a protector stronger than any gang members, so she shouldn't panic.

A quick glance in the direction of Ben showed him looking out the door, standing back out of the direct line of sight of anyone outside. This was her chance. Ben would stop anyone who came in, so she needed to make the most of the moment.

She quickly skirted the displays until she was almost at the cashier. On the way, she noticed a rack of jackets.

They were red and a cropped form-fitting style she'd never wear, just like the skinny jeans. Okay, she wasn't going to try to fit her mature figure into some jeans a teenager would be hard-pressed to pull off, but she needed a drastic visual change, so she grabbed the jacket. It wasn't very warm, and her practical soul rebelled. At least it was on sale.

She could get a new warm jacket another time. Right now, she needed to look like someone else, and this was not an Alice jacket. She found her size, held it up and then picked up one a size larger. She needed to be able to button it up comfortably at least.

There was no line at the cash register, which was good, since she felt exposed. The constant refrain of *Lord, help me, help me, help me* was going through the back of her brain as she paid with the cash she had and accepted the bag of clothing with a smile.

There was space between the cashiers and the mall. Alice found a partially shadowed section and waited for Ben.

She saw him cross the store, scanning the racks and stacks of clothing, an expression of worry etched on his face. She stepped forward, ready to wave to catch his notice. Then she remembered what he'd said about not attracting attention and almost slapped herself. She was not trained for this. She dropped her hand and leaned back against the wall. She forced herself to relax. Not totally, but her muscles were going to cramp if she was fully tensed all the time.

She trusted in God, and Ben provided the concrete reassurance of her faith.

When he was close, she stepped out of her alcove

and called softly to him. He turned to her, and she smiled at the expression of relief that crossed his face. She let him come to her, more comfortable now that she knew there was a shelter close to her. A human shelter.

"You've been shopping?" he asked, voice teasing. She could see he was experiencing a release of tension just as she was.

"I was tired of smelling like a dumpster. I also thought it would be good to change up how I look."

He nodded. "Good idea. Where were you going to change?"

"Bathroom in the mall? Is that safe?"

"Probably a good idea to get out of this store before the men following us get reinforcements and come back in to check it out again. I was sure you must have gone into the mall. Where were you?"

Alice swallowed. She'd hoped the men were gone for good. But Ben had asked a question.

"Changing room."

Ben nodded. "They may look there when they come back if they have some female help. Ready to face the mall?"

Alice took a breath, whispered a prayer and followed Ben into the mall.

The mall had never seemed hazardous before, other than to her pocketbook, and maybe to her toes at Christmas. This was different. The tension returned. She clutched her shopping bag with a death grip and found herself looking anxiously around, but she didn't know what she was looking for.

She did see a drugstore, and that gave her an idea. "I need something in there. Okay?"

He noted the store, shot a look inside it and then looked around the mall.

"Sure." He followed her in.

She went to the cosmetic section and found a small pair of scissors. Ben's brow creased, but he didn't say anything. She paid quickly and slid the scissors into her purse.

There was a mall map nearby, and they located the closest bathrooms.

Alice had latched on to the idea of changing her appearance. She felt conspicuous in the clothes she'd been wearing all day. Too many people had seen her wearing them, and she wanted to get out of them before anyone found her again.

More slowly than she liked, they made their way to the hallway with the restroom sign.

Ben leaned against the wall, a spouse waiting on his wife who could take a while. Alice gave him a wavering smile and went into the women's bathroom.

Again, on a weekday, there weren't many people around. She went into an empty stall, hung her purse up and then dived into the clothes she'd selected.

She peeled off her old faded jeans and pulled on black slacks. She changed the old sweatshirt for a nice blue shirt and sweater. She looked down. The outfit was dressy, but not bright or smart enough to attract attention. The most important thing was it was a different look from the one she'd had when they entered the mall.

She didn't want to trust in that alone. She felt her long hair that was currently pulled back into a ponytail. Henry had loved her long hair. She'd kept it long for that reason. It was a pain to dry after washing, but changing it had felt like a betrayal of him.

That decision was easy now that cutting it might help provide her with cover. She grabbed the hair tie in one hand and dug for the scissors in her bag. They were cosmetic scissors, but that was all she'd been able to find in a hurry. She took a deep breath and began to saw through the hair below the tie.

It took a couple of minutes, and the scissors pulled at the roots painfully when they got caught up, but eventually she had a handful of long brown hair in her fist. Her head felt strange, light. She pulled out the tie and shook her short strands free.

She looked at the hair in her hands, a hint of regret making her pause. It had taken her years to grow her hair out. According to Henry, it had been one of her most attractive features.

She stood up tall. Some hair was the least of her problems now. If she were caught, long hair wouldn't do anything to save her.

She couldn't hang on to it. She had to hide it where no one would find it. She considered what to do and then stuffed the hair into the bag with the old clothes she'd removed.

She pulled on the new jacket and left the safety of the stall with her purse on one shoulder and the bag in her other hand. She set both down on the counter by the sinks to wash her hands. She looked in the mirror.

Her hair looked bad. Cosmetic scissors were not designed for cutting hair. But she looked different. Drastically different.

Maybe she could convince Ben to let her stop in

a salon for half an hour to get her hair fixed. She'd look less conspicuous after a professional cut than this rough do she now had. If the men tracking her asked the salon about someone with waist-long hair coming in for a cut, she no longer fit that description. Her hair reached just about chin-level now.

A woman who came into a salon to get two feet of hair removed was noteworthy. Someone getting a bad bob touched up wouldn't be. At least, that's what she hoped.

She heard someone flushing in a stall and knew it was time to go. She stuffed her bag with the clothes and hair into the trash and raised her chin.

Ben tried not to be impatient. Alice's idea to change her appearance was a good one. Women took a little longer than men. And even though every instinct was pushing him to get away as quickly as possible, it was better to wait and do it the right way rather than rush and get caught.

Plus, he still had to figure out where they were going.

He was checking his watch again when someone stopped in front of him. He looked up, reminding himself to be polite, when he finally recognized Alice.

A different Alice.

It was almost shocking how drastically short hair changed her whole appearance. It was a little messy, but she looked younger, and the clothes she'd bought made her look like a professional on a break from work, not a woman running from her fourth attack of the day.

She looked much better than was comfortable for him right now. She smiled and looked carefree for a moment.

"You didn't recognize me!" she gloated.

Ben drew in a breath. "Nope. You look completely different."

She narrowed her gaze, biting her lip. "Any chance I could get my hair touched up?"

He blinked at her. What was she asking?

"We passed a hair salon. I know the hair is different, but it'll look sloppy if anyone really looks at me. If I could have half an hour…"

Ben almost said no. He pulled back the word at the last minute.

Alice had done a good job. She would know better than him if her hair might still give her away. And if he didn't do something about how he looked, he'd be the one who betrayed them.

He should have gotten some clothes at the first store they'd been in, but he'd been anxious to get away. If the two men in the car had passed on their descriptions, Alice wouldn't match hers any longer.

He would. He needed to either change his appearance or stay away from her. There was no one else to watch her, so option two was out.

That shouldn't make him feel good.

They'd already had close calls when being near Alice had distracted him. He couldn't afford another. Alice couldn't afford another.

He had to rein in this attraction before it cost Alice her life.

NINE

"We can take a look at the salon."

She smiled in response. He liked that smile. He wanted to give her more things to smile about.

But that was the problem. He had to be objective. The priority now wasn't smiles—it was safety. If he compromised her safety for a momentary bit of happiness, he'd never forgive himself.

He was second-guessing his decisions. He couldn't do that.

Alice was unaware of his conflict and led them to the salon. He forced himself to examine it without looking at her face or considering her feelings.

He'd already decided that if there was one open room where passersby could see the customers being worked on, it would be too much of a risk.

Fortunately, it wasn't. There was a reception area, and the hair stations were behind a wall and out of view.

Since it was midweek in February, things were quiet, and there was even a hairdresser available immediately.

Ben assessed Alice's idea with as much objectivity as he could. Alice should be safe here for the moment.

She wouldn't be in view if anyone passed by in the mall, and she didn't match the description anyone would have for her. Plus, he knew exactly where she was.

He nodded at her but refused to return her smile. "I'm going to grab a change of clothes, too. I'll be back as quickly as I can."

Alice looked panicked but drew in a breath. "You'll be quick?"

He nodded again. "If not, you have the money. I'm going to give you a phone number. It should get you through to someone who can connect to Chris's team. You need to call in before he'll testify, and if you tell them you're in trouble, they'll help you."

Her worried gaze met his. "The mole?"

He shook his head. "I just don't know. Use the number as a last resort."

Ben hadn't planned on buying new wardrobes when he took out the cash from the bank machine. He had to travel a little farther down the mall to find a store that carried less expensive clothing to get himself a change of pants and shirt he could afford. He found a cheap jacket on sale, but it took almost all the cash he had left on hand.

He needed to find a solution. A place to keep Alice safe. And it had to be cheap.

No problem. Right.

He kept his eyes peeled as he made his way to a bathroom to change into his new clothes. A glance in the mirror made him aware that even with the new outfit his face was recognizable. Mostly, he thought, it was the hair.

He'd never paid much attention to his looks, and since his wife Laura's death back when he was still a rookie, there hadn't been anyone to nag him into getting haircuts. When it got long enough that his commanding officer made comments, he'd stop at a barber.

At the rural detachment in Lychford, he was the top dog, and no one had told him to get a haircut. While he was finding his feet there, determined to do a good job so that no one suspected the reason for his presence, haircuts hadn't been at the top of his list of things to do.

Still, if he wanted to deflect attention, he was going to have to spend a bit more of the shrinking cash stash and get cleaned up.

When he got back to the salon, Alice was still safely behind the partition. Relieved, he sat down in a seat where he could keep his eye on anyone passing by. In fact, thanks to the mirror on the wall, he could see people coming in either direction all while watching the space where Alice would appear when she was done.

He'd picked up a magazine to augment his cover, and that gave him the second he needed to put the periodical in front of his face when he saw faces he recognized coming toward the salon in the mirror's reflection.

It wasn't the two men from earlier. No, Ben recognized these two from his time on a task force a few years ago. They belonged to the same gang as the man Chris was going to testify against.

The men moved slowly down the mall, scanning the faces of the people going by, as well as looking into each store they passed. Some stores, they entered.

Ben was grateful he'd changed his clothing. Unless they saw his face from behind the magazine, he shouldn't be recognized, and they should be safe.

But what if they came in?

When one of the pair went into the candle store across the way, and the other stood looking toward the opposite end of the mall, Ben got up and walked back around the partition.

He thought he felt eyes burning into the back of his exposed and vulnerable head, but no one came into the salon after them. The tension eased as he made it around the partition and knew he was no longer at risk of being seen.

He checked for a back door and saw there was a small hallway opposite him with doors Ben hoped they used to take out garbage and bring in supplies. Disappearing out a service entrance wasn't his first choice. It would only be a matter of time before the hairdresser shared the information with the police or anyone asking if she'd seen a couple behaving strangely. They'd have to come up with a convincing reason for her to keep quiet, especially if someone with a badge was asking questions.

The gang knew Alice had come into the mall. If the gang couldn't find her here, would the mole be able to send police reinforcements?

Having assessed the exit, Ben turned to the woman he was determined to protect.

"Hey, sis. You done yet?"

He hoped a brother and sister would be less memorable. If anyone inquired about a woman with long hair, they'd be less likely to hear about Alice, the woman with short hair who came in with her brother.

The hairdresser swung the cape from Alice. Ben stopped, at a loss for words.

Alice had looked different once she cut her long ponytail off in the mall bathroom, but the change now was amazing. Her hair was shorter than his. It wisped around her head, light, playful and young.

She looked— Ben cut off that thought. He needed to focus on his job.

Alice turned and looked at him. Was she looking for approval? Or reassurance?

Ben forced himself to put on his cop blinders. He needed to look at the path ahead, nothing else.

"Looks good, sis." He saw her start to frown and then blink as comprehension hit.

"Thanks, bro."

"You know, you were right. I need to get my hair cut as well so you don't show me up."

She turned to her hairdresser. "Hey, Rita. I don't suppose you have any more time right now? My brother is looking kind of scruffy."

Rita did have time. Ben debated between the undoubtedly higher expense of having Rita cut his hair versus trying to find a barber before someone spotted them.

He went with safety.

Rita wrapped a cape around his neck and stuck his head in the sink for a wash. He hated being less aware of his surroundings for those minutes, but he didn't want to attract attention by resisting.

Once he was in the chair, Alice made suggestions on how Rita should cut her "brother's" hair. Alice distracted Rita by discussing in boring detail the wedding they were supposedly attending this weekend.

While she and Rita debated the incomprehensible difference between peach and apricot when it came to table linens, Ben was able to concentrate on their surroundings again. He was the one who heard someone enter the front of the salon and told Rita. While he and Alice sat behind the partition, Rita went around to the counter.

"I'm looking for my mother. We were supposed to meet somewhere around here, but I can't find her. Have you seen a woman with long brown hair, brown jacket, about so tall?"

Ben didn't recognize the voice, but he knew it was one of the gang.

They should have said something to Rita. Told her not to mention them. He was sitting in the chair, hair partially cut, his new jacket with Alice on the next seat.

Alice was staring at him with wide eyes. He put a finger to his lips and pointed to the rear door. If Rita gave them away, or if the man insisted on coming around the corner, they'd have to make a run for it.

Ben unwrapped the cape Rita had wound around his neck to protect him from bits of hair falling on his clothes, making sure to pull the Velcro apart slowly enough to avoid making noise.

"I work in the back, so I don't see very many people. Was she going to get her hair cut or colored?"

Was Rita helping them, or just telling the truth? Ben could imagine that the man out there didn't look trustworthy, or safe.

Alice passed him his coat. He slipped it on, and they walked slowly and quietly toward the back. He saw a beanie sitting on a counter and quickly grabbed it.

"I don't know. Maybe. Did a woman with long brown hair come in here and cut her hair? Maybe with a guy?"

"No, I haven't had anyone with long hair in today."

Ben put his hand on the doorknob of the rear exit. He wasn't sure where this would lead, but it would be away from the gang member out front.

Alice shook her head. He frowned. She jerked her head toward the salon and reached for her purse.

"Then you won't mind letting me see," the man out front said, his voice getting louder. They could hear Rita's protests, but there was no time.

Ben opened the door, grabbed Alice's hand and pulled her through the doorway. He slipped through himself, closing the door and latching it as quickly and quietly as he could.

They were now in a drab and narrow hallway with doors opening off to one side. There was a corridor off to the left, and Ben broke into a run, reaching for Alice's arm as he did so. He ended up with her hand in his, and she followed him around the corner.

A sign indicated where the stairs were, and they followed the arrow.

Ben could hear footsteps behind them. "Don't look back," he told her.

For just a few minutes, Alice had been able to forget she was on the run. It had been fun to see her locks dropping on the floor and to feel lighter with each cut. But that good feeling was all gone. Now, she remembered why she'd needed to cut her hair. She needed to hide. The gang was desperate to stop Chris from testifying, and one of the gang members was right behind them.

Ben had one of her hands in his, racing down the stairs. Alice didn't have time to watch where her feet were going and prayed she wouldn't trip and fall. She didn't think she'd be able to get back up again if that happened.

At the foot of the stairs, Ben turned toward a sign for the washrooms. He passed her the beanie hat he'd picked up somewhere, freeing her hand. Alice pulled it down over her new haircut with a mental wince. It had looked so nice.

Once they neared the washrooms, people looked up as they ran around the corner. Ben slowed to a walk and joined a group of people heading back out into the mall. He leaned down and put his mouth by her ear.

"We need to get out of the mall. I think our best bet might be the subway. It's harder to watch the platforms than the doors in and out of the mall. You still have your day pass?"

Alice had stashed it in the pocket of her purse.

She nodded. "Queen Station or Dundas?"

Ben shot a glance behind them instead of answering.

"Is he still there?"

Ben moved them down a side aisle.

"I don't know what he looks like, but there's someone back there keeping an eye on us."

Alice swallowed. She'd hoped they'd gotten lost in the crowd.

"I have an idea. Will you do exactly what I tell you? We're going to need to make some last-second moves."

Alice had been trusting him this far. She nodded.

They were now in a crowd of people heading toward

the entrance to the Queen Street subway. They used their day passes to get through the gates.

Alice desperately wanted to check if the man following them had been held up by not having a pass, but she followed Ben's instructions and kept looking forward.

Ben led her to the side of the tracks for the northbound cars.

"Did we lose him?"

Ben glanced over. "No, I see him coming now. I don't know if he's sure we're his quarry or just a couple who stiffed the hair salon, but I want him to see us get on the subway. Just don't let him see your haircut. I'm hoping that surprise is still something we have in reserve."

Alice frowned. "What if he gets on the subway, too?"

Ben's mouth quirked. "That's why we have to be ready to move quickly."

Alice thought it would be better if no one knew they'd left the mall at all, but Ben had a sense of purpose about him. He had a plan, and while she'd like to know it, she decided to trust him.

She would.

The train rushed into the station. It was now late afternoon, Alice realized, and the subway was filling up. The doors slid open, and some people slipped out, but there were more bodies interested in getting on than off.

Ben held Alice's elbow, and they were the last ones on the subway car. The telltale pings announcing that the doors were about to close gave everyone notice, and Ben suddenly jerked her out of the car. At the very last second, he pulled her back in, and the doors slid closed in front of her, missing her nose by inches.

TEN

Alice opened her mouth, but Ben gave a terse jerk of his head, and she closed her mouth again.

The train slipped into the tunnel, and Alice could see their reflections in the door of the car. It wasn't long before the train started to slow again, and she heard a muffled voice announce they were approaching Dundas Station.

As soon as the doors slid open, Ben nudged her forward. Then, hand still on her elbow, he led her off the platform. Instead of exiting the station, however, he led them to the southbound side.

A train pulled in, and they ran to get on board.

Alice thought she saw his plan. They'd be expected at the northbound stations, and those would be watched. But they would be going south. She hoped Ben had a destination in mind.

The voice announced their arrival back at the Queen Street station. The doors slid open, and a few people got out. Ben was watching the platform, and as the door-closing chime started, he shoved them both off the train.

They were back where they had started.

Alice felt her brow furrow.

Ben headed off the platform, tagging Alice along behind him.

Just before exiting through the turnstiles, he stopped to lean against the wall, his eyes on the people entering the station.

"I'm sorry I couldn't explain earlier, but I didn't want anyone to overhear."

He had his voice pitched low, so low that Alice had to lean in to catch his words. No one passing by would be able to understand.

"I thought of leaving by subway, and when you mentioned the two stations, I hoped we could pull this off. The guy who followed us must be looking for you. I don't think he saw your haircut, so that means your disguise will still work.

"He didn't get on the northbound train with us, so he'd have had to catch the next train to try to follow. Either that, or he'd have to head somewhere with cell reception to let the rest of the people looking for you know that we're heading north.

"We've been seen heading out of the mall. Anyone watching for us should keep looking all the way north. The one place they won't be looking for us—"

Alice grinned.

"The mall here."

Ben nodded. "This is our chance to grab some food and make a plan."

Alice's stomach gurgled, and she bit her lip. "Obviously, I'm on board for that. But there's something we need to do first."

Ben raised his brows.

"Let's find a family restroom. You've had half a haircut. I think you'd better wear the beanie now, or people will notice you. Those scissors I bought should do the job, unless you want to go back to the salon so we can pay Rita?"

She hated that the hairdresser must think they were thieves.

Ben turned and gripped her hand. "Alice, once you're safe, I'll go back and pay her what we owe her and give her the biggest tip she's ever seen, but right now, your safety comes first."

He was right. She knew that. It still bothered her.

She nodded. "I want to leave her a tip, too."

Ben looked around. "Right now, we're doing pretty well. Let's hit the food court. Then we can figure out where we're headed next."

They stopped for ten minutes in a family restroom, and Alice did her best with the scissors to make Ben's hair look planned, rather than an accident. When that was done, the scissors were barely functioning, but at least Ben's hair wouldn't attract any attention. Ben left the room first, and when it was safe, he motioned for her to come out. They followed a crowd of teenagers heading to the food court.

Then they were in the midst of it. The smells of grease, spices and coffee teased their way through the tables.

It felt wrong. They had who knew how many people looking for them, and sitting to eat a meal was anti-climactic. Banal. But since she was relying so much on Ben, it would be smart to provide him with food to keep going. And she should eat as well, so she wouldn't be a weak link that left them in jeopardy.

"What do you want?" Ben nodded at the various vendors.

"I don't know that I care much."

"Is there anything you can't eat? Allergies, etc.?"

Alice shook her head.

Ben led her to a Thai counter. "We need protein and some slow carbs to tide us over."

Alice wondered how long it would have to tide them until but didn't ask. She wasn't sure she wanted an honest answer, and Ben had been blunt with her so far.

Once Ben had placed their order on a tray, they found a quiet corner. Alice was glad to sit and drink some water and pretend again, for a few minutes, that this was just a stop in the food court, a break in a day of shopping, rather than a day on the run.

For Pete's sake, she wasn't the kind of person to be on the run.

She noticed Ben watching one of the TVs scattered around. His posture was stiff. She turned to the TV and saw her picture.

It was an old picture. She wasn't sure exactly where they'd found it, but she had her hair long and tumbling over her shoulders in it. It didn't look like the woman she'd seen in the mirror at the salon.

She was grateful.

Then she noticed Ben's photo placed beside hers on the monitor.

It was an official photo of Ben in his police uni-form. He didn't look exactly the same, not with his new haircut and the gray that was prevalent now, but he was much more recognizable.

The feed underneath indicated they were wanted for questioning in regards to the attack on police officers at St. Mike's hospital earlier today.

The photos and the information scrolling beneath them all made it look like *they* were the ones suspected of carrying out the attack, rather than the victims.

Alice's appetite fled.

"Shouldn't we get out of here?" she whispered to the man beside her.

His lips were gripped in a narrow line. She saw his gaze travel over the people around them, most of whom were absorbed in their own conversations and ignoring the TVs.

"Yeah, we need to go. But we're going to be casual, not in a rush, just putting away our food. We need to be extra careful now."

"Why?"

Ben looked at her, brows heavy. He was worried—it was there in every expression and gesture.

He gestured at the TV still broadcasting the twenty-four-hour news. "That change in message didn't come from just anyone. Any cop getting that message is being told I'm a problem, that I've gone rogue and have you as a hostage or something similar. That means that anyone on the force is going to apprehend me first and ask questions later. If we're caught, I'm off for interrogation, and you're taken into protection—but we know that the protection isn't going to keep you safe."

Alice swallowed over a dry throat.

"I can't risk contacting anyone I know in the force.

Everyone there is now going to be looking for us. The mole must be someone pretty high up. He's got power. And all of it is focused against us."

Alice drew in a shuddering breath.

"It's a good thing we've got power on our side, too."

Ben shot her a glance.

"I have faith, Ben. And I'm praying. I believe that offsets any power your mole has."

She waited, unsure if he would scoff. She didn't know whether he was a believer now, or whether he might have been in the past.

"We can use any help we can get. But my backup plans aren't going to work right now, so we should find someplace less public to figure out our next move." Ben scanned the food court one more time.

"We'll stop in the restrooms since we're not sure when we'll get another chance."

Ben had finished most of his meal. He slid Alice's plate onto his tray, stacking their dishes. He passed her the extra water bottles he'd ordered, and she put them into her purse. He pointed out the direction of the washrooms, and they agreed to meet up outside the doors.

Ben was out first. He leaned against the wall, watching the people passing by, searching for familiar faces or anyone who looked suspicious. A security guard approached, and a niggling memory made Ben's stomach knot.

Alice had fixed his hair, and he looked different from the photos the news had broadcast. Someone who didn't know him would probably not recognize him right away, but this guy knew him. The security guard was a former cop. He and Ben spent years working out of the same station.

To make matters worse, this guy had never liked Ben and had probably been thrilled to find out Ben was in trouble.

He saw the moment the guard recognized him. The man blinked, opened his mouth and then reached for his radio. Ben couldn't let this guy make that call. Making a move would draw attention, but if the guard got through on that radio, they were exposed anyway.

The guard wasn't expecting a tackle. There weren't a lot of people back here by the restrooms, but those who stood nearby scattered. Ben and the guard hit the floor before the man managed to transmit anything on the radio. He wasn't that much older than Ben, but Ben was heavier, more experienced and much more motivated.

The guard's eyes went wide with panic as Ben pinned him to the floor. Ben needed to disable him quickly and prevent him from calling this in as long as possible. A couple of people turned back to see what was going on, and from the corner of his eye, he caught a glimpse of Alice's coat.

He didn't want anyone to notice her, to remember her with him.

"This is for Rita!" he yelled, hoping Alice would catch the hint. Then he moved his knees onto the man's arms, whispered, "Sorry", and banged the man's head on the floor hard enough to knock him unconscious.

His guts twisted. This was a horrible thing to do to someone, but he knew there was no way to reason with this man, not in the seconds he had before the radio call would go through. He grabbed the man's radio, wallet and weapons.

"Call 911!" he yelled and rose from the limp form on the ground, probably confusing the people who'd seen what he'd done. New people rushing to see what was going on would interpret the scene a little differently based on Ben's latest actions.

More people rushed over, and Ben managed to slip into the gathering crowd, letting them push him back until he was free to turn and walk away.

He hoped Alice had understood the message he'd tried to send her. He stopped at the end of the food court, leaned against a wall and surveyed the area. He didn't see any emergency personnel yet, but with this number of witnesses, someone would call, and the guard would be taken care of.

He hoped the man would be out long enough to allow them to make their escape but that he hadn't been seriously injured. Ben didn't know how long they had, so they needed to leave. Now.

Two more minutes of observation to make sure no one was tracking him felt like an hour. He dropped the radio and gun into the nearest garbage bin, then he made his way to where he was hoping to find Alice.

The salon was closed. He glanced inside, but there was no one in the waiting area. Had the man from the gang come back and taken Rita somewhere to get more details about the couple whose hair she'd cut? Or had she been frightened by the man and left?

He hoped it was the latter.

Meanwhile, he had no idea where Alice was.

ELEVEN

Alice's knees almost buckled when she saw Ben in front of the salon. When she'd heard him say something about Rita, she'd known he meant to meet there.

She'd popped into the candle shop across from the salon to watch for him from there, in case anyone else came looking for her. She'd sniffed enough candles to numb her sense of smell for days when she saw Ben.

It probably hadn't been more than a few minutes, but it felt like hours. She'd tried to think of a backup plan in case Ben wasn't able to get back here, but she'd only gotten as far as praying. She had no idea what to do in a situation like this.

She exercised caution and watched to make sure no one was following Ben before she left the store. His expression was blank, but she recognized he was covering the panic in his eyes. When he spotted her, relief washed over his face.

"Hi, brother. Was just looking at candles for a wedding present."

Ben smiled at her. "I think I'm done shopping for today."

Alice struggled to maintain her smile. How quickly did they need to leave? "Okay, I can come back later for anything else."

"Great. You know I've never cared much for shopping, anyway." She followed his lead, walking south toward the same mall entrance they'd come in.

Ben stopped to look in a store window just before the walkway to the department store that adjoined the mall. They were one floor up from the street. Alice was puzzled but turned to look in the window with him.

"Do you see the guys standing by the walkway?" he said, voice low.

Alice pretended to check the price on an item in the window. "With the leather jackets?"

"They're looking for us."

Alice didn't question how he knew. "So what's the plan?"

After the number of times she'd asked him that, she should just put it on a plaque.

She could hear the frustration in his voice. "I'd hoped they'd think we'd left. I don't know if our make-overs are good enough to get us through, and I don't want to risk it if I can help it. I don't want to go back to the subway again."

Ben nodded, and she followed him down the nearby stairs to ground level. They avoided the food court, heading further back into the mall.

He nodded to an exit down a hallway, currently filled with end of day commuters. There was a sign, letters in blocks: The PATH.

The PATH was an underground network of shops, restaurants and other services all under downtown Toronto. It was a rabbit warren connected to the streets above, easily confusing anyone not gifted with a great sense of direction or a mental map of the city. On the rare times Alice had been in Toronto, she'd never used it.

Ben growled. "Don't look to your left. I think some of our cousins are over that way."

Alice wished he hadn't said that. She had an over-whelming urge to look now. She wanted to see what the danger was.

"I'm going to drop behind you. They're probably looking for two people. Your haircut should still con-fuse them. I'll catch up to you as soon as it's safe."

Alice had to bite her lip to keep the words back. She wanted to ask Ben not to leave her. He'd become her safety, her rock. She was trusting him to keep her safe. Even though she hadn't known him before this morning, the idea of being alone now was terrifying.

As she found herself moving forward with the crowd, avoiding looking to the left, she remembered Ben wasn't the only help she had.

Yea, though I walk through the valley of the shadow of death, she prayed.

She didn't know where God was leading her, but she would trust He would take care of her now and always. She straightened her spine and held her head high, walking forward confidently as though she were just another office worker heading home. She'd follow the crowd until Ben joined her, and if they weren't able to reconnect, she'd trust her heavenly Father to lead her.

There was a corner coming up. Some people were turning right, some going straight. Ben wasn't here to direct her, and she didn't know where she was. One of the signs had Union Station as a destination.

She knew Union Station. It had subways, GO trains, VIA Rail. There were a lot of ways to get out of Union Station, and a lot of ways to get in. Surely, they'd be watching for her there? She turned in the opposite direction and kept walking.

Ben saw the watchers on the walkway run their gazes over Alice and keep moving. They watched the couples passing by, and Ben's shoulders relaxed. Alice was past them now.

She was the prize they were looking for, and she was safe for the moment. She was also the one who looked drastically different, so she was less likely to be recognized than he was. Whatever cash they had left after purchasing clothes and haircuts and food was with her.

Ben remembered the wallet he'd kept, the one belonging to the security guard. He needed to check if there was some cash in there.

Ben didn't want to be caught. If another cop brought him in, he'd face some difficulties, but if the gang caught him, it wouldn't be pleasant. He hoped he could hold out against what would undoubtedly be a physical interrogation to see if he knew where Alice was. At least, that's all they could do to him. Unlike Chris, he didn't have anyone they could use to coerce him. Not anymore.

As he passed the gang members, he hunched over a bit, allowed his tiredness to show, trying not to look like a cop. The change to his physical appearance was not as drastic as Alice's, so he had to make up for it in other ways.

He kept walking with the crowd, not looking anywhere around him. He felt eyeballs on him, but then the feeling passed. He was through. The two men were still focusing on couples. He saw them check the screen of their phones, as he paused to read a poster.

Then he heard a voice shout, "Hey, you!"

It could be anyone calling out to a person in the crowd, but he didn't think so. He couldn't risk it.

He didn't want to run—there were too many people, and it would attract too much attention. But he moved quickly, weaving around other people, looking for the tallest in the crowd to keep himself hidden.

First chance he got, he turned to the stairs to the external doors.

He knew Alice was going to stay in the PATH. At least, he was pretty sure she would. They hadn't talked about leaving there. He wanted to lead any pursuers away from her, and outside was away. He pushed the doors open and went through.

The sudden cold was shocking. He walked as quickly as he could down the street. He didn't think anyone was directly behind him, so he headed into the lobby of the nearest high-rise. There were a lot of workers all starting to head home, and Ben found a corner and drew himself back out of sight. He focused on the door of the building in case someone entered.

Ben glanced out the window and saw the two men who'd been watching people leave the mall via the hallway to the PATH. He didn't know if the men had spotted him, or whether his hasty exit had caught their attention, but they'd followed him out of the mall and were now on the street. They headed toward the building he was in.

Of course. It was the closest.

He pulled back and looked around the lobby, checking for escape routes. The doorway he'd come in through was large and unobstructed. There was an escalator back down to the PATH, but he'd be exposed if he headed that way, and he didn't want to lead them to where Alice was.

There were hallways to a bank of elevators currently disgorging workers done for the day, and Ben considered whether he could sneak away while they searched the lobby.

He drew a long breath, trying to slow his racing heart, and left his corner. He didn't turn around, didn't look, but he didn't walk slowly, either. He headed quickly to where he saw a group of suited people exiting an elevator car and slipped inside just as the doors were closing. He was the only one inside.

This car was an express and only went to the top twenty floors, bypassing floors two through twenty-five. He punched buttons for every floor, like a kid playing with the numbers. Anyone watching the numbers displayed in the lobby would have no idea which floor he was exiting on, but he still had no idea how to get back to Alice.

He could try the stairs to get back down, but if he were them, he'd have called in reinforcements to watch those. The elevator stopped on the thirty-second floor. There was no one waiting. Ben hopped out, unwilling to continue rising with the elevator. Instead, he pushed the down button once his car had continued to the upper floors.

He was risking a lot. He couldn't get caught, but he had to get back to Alice, which meant he couldn't hide out here. The door pinged, signaling a car going down. It was about half-full with office workers. Ben stepped on and did his best to move toward the back of the car, and with the stop on the next floor, he allowed himself to be pushed farther back by the people getting on.

On the last floor, before the express drop to the lobby, there were two people watching the car, two men who didn't get on. Ben bent his knees, keeping himself out of view. By this point, he was against the wall, hidden by bodies. He held his breath, and the doors closed. The elevator started to fall, but Ben's stomach was already at the bottom.

The elevator stopped on a mezzanine level, and almost half the people got out. Ben was no longer hidden, but no one was watching the elevator car. Perhaps they were all in the lobby or on the upper floors looking for him there?

He quickly stepped off the car just before the doors slid closed and looked down to the lobby. He caught the movement of two men near the doors, and one pointed up at him. They made a call and started moving in the direction of the stairs to the mezzanine.

Ben moved for the walkway to the next building.

This time, he knew for sure he had their attention.

He walked quickly but didn't run. He made sure his coat was unbuttoned, hoping to change some of his appearance when he was out of their direct line of sight. Once around the corner at the end of the walkway, he removed his coat, tucked it under his arm and headed down to the lobby where he would have more options. Stepping off the escalator, he saw a hat on the floor. A quick glance showed no one looking, so he reached down, picked it up and shoved it down over his hair.

He'd done what he could to make himself look different, and he stepped on the escalator that continued down to the PATH. Once there, he found a sheltered spot and waited.

After a few minutes, when he saw no one following, the band around his chest eased. As far as he could tell, he'd lost them.

Unfortunately, he'd lost Alice, as well.

TWELVE

Alice was resolved to trust God in this situation, but she was beginning to panic. She truly was on her own. She'd seen no sign of Ben for at least twenty minutes.

Maybe she should have followed the directions to Union Station. She'd gone down one passageway of the PATH and ended up facing steps to the outside. Ben hadn't said anything about going outside. It was really cold out there, and the temperatures were dropping as darkness fell. Maybe there was a car out there with members of the gang inside it, like there had been where they'd entered the mall.

Ben was the one who could identify who was dangerous. Alice wouldn't recognize the danger until she was in it.

She turned around and retraced her steps, looking anxiously for a glimpse of Ben. Her palms were sweating even though she'd stuffed her gloves in her bag and unbuttoned her jacket. She could feel her heart beating faster. She cast nervous glances around her, desperately anxious to see Ben. When a woman passing her frowned, Alice realized she was attracting attention. The one thing she couldn't afford.

She found a bench tucked into a corner, sat down, and willed her body to stop panicking. She rested her head on her hands, hiding her face from the people passing by. She heard Ben's voice in her memories.

They'll hurt you, not fatally, and send him proof to put more pressure on him.

Someone in your position would never be seen again.

Your son witnessed a murder. So that's not a line these people are afraid to cross.

Her fingers trembled in her hair. She was afraid. God felt out of reach.

All day, she'd been running on adrenaline, but she'd had Ben's presence to comfort her. Now, it looked like she was on her own, and she was petrified. She'd relied on Ben more than she knew. Maybe too much.

She had a small amount of cash. She had a phone she couldn't use in case it was traced. She had a lightweight jacket and gloves that wouldn't keep her warm for long in the freezing temperatures outside. And with all of those problems, she had to keep away from the police and this gang until tomorrow. Or would she need to stay hidden until Chris was done testifying?

If she didn't call Chris, he wouldn't testify. The bad guys would win, but at least she and Chris would be alive.

She was distracted by the sound of a familiar voice nearby. It was a man, but it wasn't Ben.

"Do you think they're still together?"

The PATH was noisy, but she could still hear the people talking around the corner from her bench.

"Moody and Bones spotted him in one of the high-rises on his own. Maybe he hid her someplace, or maybe they split up."

Could they be talking about Ben and her?

"So what are we doing here?"

"We're looking for her. Maybe him. Moody got a shot of him with his phone camera, but he thinks the guy's on street level. We're supposed to look for any woman on her own. She's probably not even here, but after we missed her at the house, this is where we're stuck."

"If she's here, we'll find her. We don't have to be careful anymore. Doesn't matter if anyone sees us, as long as we get her."

Alice could scarcely breathe. She recognized the voices. They belonged to the two guys who'd been at her house. They were looking for any woman on her own, and they were just around the corner from her. If they came over this way, it was all over.

The only thing protecting her from capture, torture and probable death was her haircut.

It might not be enough.

A cold started spreading from somewhere inside, moving to her limbs. She was frozen and still, like a small animal hoping to evade a large predator. She had no defenses.

Suddenly, through the panic, came a verse from memory.

The God of my rock, in Him I will trust: He is my shield, and the horn of my salvation, my high tower, and my refuge, my savior—Thou savest me from violence.

She did have a defense. The best one.

The thoughts she'd been having, the ones that told her to be full of fear, they weren't from God, and she shouldn't listen to them. In this moment, when she had nothing else to depend on, she still had her faith.

Thank You, Lord. Help me trust You.

She took a deep breath, wiped her palms on her pants and got to her feet.

Though I walk through the valley of the shadow of death, I will fear no evil.

She was distracted enough that she didn't notice someone coming in from the street until she bumped into him.

"I'm so sorry," she said.

The boy—no, a man—was around Chris's age. He was wearing a hat with the logo of the local basketball team and the jersey of one of the players, but she didn't know if it was a current or past player. Neither she, nor her family had ever been big basketball fans.

"No problem," he responded with a smile. From the corner of her eye, she saw a man come around the corner. Desperation, or something else, inspired her.

She stepped beside him. "Can I ask a favor?"

His expression turned wary.

"There's a guy who's been following me." That was technically true.

"I wondered if I could walk with you so he thinks I'm with someone and he leaves me alone."

That was also the truth. No one was looking for a woman her age with a young man. Would it be enough?

"Absolutely." He offered her his arm. It was sweet. "Do you have someplace safe to go?"

Loyal Readers
FREE BOOKS Voucher

We're giving away THOUSANDS of FREE BOOKS

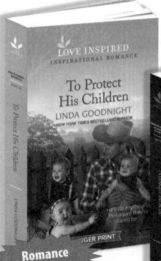

Romance

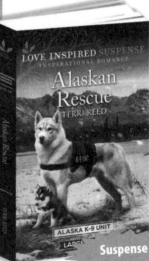

Suspense

Don't Miss Out! Send for Your Free Books Today!

Get up to 4
FREE FABULOUS BOOKS
You Love!

To thank you for being a loyal reader we'd like to send you up to 4 FREE BOOKS, absolutely free.

Just write "YES" on the Loyal Reader Voucher and we'll send you up to 4 Free Books and Free Mystery Gifts, altogether worth over $20, as a way of saying thank you for being a loyal reader.

Try **Love Inspired® Romance Larger-Print** books and fall in love with inspirational romances that take you on an uplifting journey of faith, forgiveness and hope.

Try **Love Inspired® Suspense Larger-Print** books where courage and optimism unite in stories of faith and love in the face of danger.

Or **TRY BOTH!**

We are so glad you love the books as much as we do and can't wait to send you great new books.

So don't miss out, return your Loyal Reader Voucher Today!

Pam Powers

LOYAL READER
FREE BOOKS VOUCHER

YES! I Love Reading, please send me up to 4 FREE BOOKS and Free Mystery Gifts from the series I select.

Just write in "YES" on the dotted line below then return this card today and we'll send your free books & gifts asap!

➡ ⸺ YES ⸺ ⬅

Which do you prefer?

☐ **Love Inspired® Romance Larger-Print**
122/322 IDL GRJD

☐ **Love Inspired® Suspense Larger-Print**
107/307 IDL GRJD

☐ **BOTH**
122/322 & 107/307
IDL GRJP

FIRST NAME

LAST NAME

ADDRESS

APT.#

CITY

STATE/PROV.

ZIP/POSTAL CODE

EMAIL ☐ Please check this box if you would like to receive newsletters and promotional emails from Harlequin Enterprises ULC and its affiliates. You can unsubscribe anytime.

LI/SLI-520-LR21

Alice was breathing quickly, doing her best to ignore the men she'd heard talking now that she was at the corner and they would be able to see her. It took a moment for the young man's words to connect with her brain.

Somewhere safe to go? No, she didn't. She almost told him that and asked him to help her, but he was asking about now, not offering a place of refuge for the whole night. And even if he were willing to offer her somewhere to stay, she didn't know him. She'd have to explain a lot to make him understand, and he might not get it. He might insist on involving the police.

Only a few hours ago, she'd thought she could rely on the justice system to keep her safe, and that had resulted in people getting hurt at the hospital. She couldn't risk anyone else's safety. Right now, Ben was the only person she trusted.

She walked in the same direction this young man was headed, and it was enough to get her past the two men looking for her, but her new protector was worried.

"Should we call the cops?" he asked.

That was the instinctive response of most people. It had been her response this morning.

She put on a smile. "No, no, don't worry. I'm meeting a friend. I'll be safe with him."

She would be, if she found him. If not, God would protect her. He'd sent Ben to her and then provided this young man to help her in a crunch.

He was frowning. "You sure?"

"Absolutely. I appreciate the help you've provided, but I'm good."

He still looked concerned. He was a good kid.

"Where are you meeting him?"

What should she say? She didn't know the PATH well, and she didn't want to spend too much time on her own. The young man's face showed his worry, and as she looked at him, she noticed what he was wearing. A lot of people around them were wearing similar team gear, and it gave Alice an idea.

"There's a game tonight?"

He nodded.

"I'm meeting my friend at the arena," she said.

That would work. It would get her safely away from the PATH, and then she could figure out how to find Ben. He was on street level, according to those men. God would need to lead her, because she had no idea what to do.

"Cool," the young man said. "That's where I'm meeting my friends." He then told her all about the upcoming game, the visiting team, their strengths and weaknesses, and what the home team needed to do to win. Alice let it flow over her head. She watched the other people around them, looking for Ben or anyone else who might be looking for her.

She saw a couple of police officers and reluctantly kept herself alongside her new friend.

Not long before they reached the arena, her companion found his friends.

"You wanna come with us?"

She smiled. "No, thank you, I'll be fine now. No sign of that guy. Tell your mother she did a good job raising you."

A flush stained his cheeks. "Ah, anyone would have done it."

"But you did."

"Are you and your friend going to the game?"

Alice blinked. "Um, I'm not sure."

If she found Ben, she didn't think he'd want to attend a ball game.

He pulled out his wallet and pulled out two tickets.

"Robby won some tickets to better seats, so I have these extras. Take them," he insisted when she'd started to shake her head.

"If you don't want them, maybe you can find someone else who does. Pay it forward."

If she didn't find Ben, she could take these tickets and hide out in the arena for a while. This might be where God was leading her.

"Thank you. I will."

It was hard to let him go, but she didn't want to get him in trouble. He'd already helped so much.

Now she had two tickets to a basketball game, but no Ben, and no idea what to do next.

Ben noticed his lace was untied, and that was what saved him.

He stopped to tie up the lace, and when he looked up and ahead, he saw a couple of uniformed officers. He'd almost run right into them.

They were standing at each side of the main hallway through the PATH that headed to Union Station. They were watching the people pass by, scanning each face.

They could be here for many reasons, but Ben

couldn't risk it. He turned and slowly traced his way back until he found a side exit that led up to the street.

The street exit could be watched. He thought he'd diverted attention to the streets and away from the PATH, but the presence of the two policemen gave him reason to believe all possibilities were being examined.

He had no idea what to do. If he went through the PATH to find Alice, the police would see him. If he went out this door, the gang or police could see him. At least he couldn't give any information about Alice's current whereabouts, because he had no idea where she was.

It was time to make a decision.

A group of businessmen pushed past him, and he joined their wake as they went up the steps and out the door. The air was piercing cold, but he'd take that.

Then he heard someone say, "There he is."

Ben didn't take the time to see who it was, or to verify they were after him. He saw a bus about to take off from the curb, and he leaped on, digging for his day pass. The vehicle was packed, and there was barely room for him, but it was enough.

The roads were clogged this time of day, exhaust gas floating up from the many vehicles. The bus was caught up in traffic and slow. Whoever was after him would be able to catch up soon.

The bus slowed at the next intersection. Ben looked back. He saw two men pushing through the crowds on the sidewalk. With the light about to change, he was stuck. They'd be even with him in a moment.

But the bus driver was aggressive, and he took the late amber, pushing through as the light turned red.

The men were stuck waiting for the light to change again and were talking on their phones, so Ben expected someone at one of the next stops.

He jumped off as soon as the bus pulled to a stop and spotted a subway entrance just around the corner. Ben bolted down the stairs, doing his best to avoid other commuters.

At this time of day, the northbound trains would be packed, and Ben might not be able to get on the first one. Southbound trains were much less crowded since people were heading home at the end of the workday.

Ben took the southbound stairs, and just as he landed on the platform, a train slowed to a stop. Not one to second-guess this opportunity, Ben tried to regulate his breathing and stepped onto the train.

The familiar pings sounded, and the doors slid closed. And as the train pulled out, he saw two uniformed sets of legs coming down the escalator to the platform.

He'd escaped the watchers. He was almost weak with relief. Now, he just had to find Alice. Most of the people on the train with him were wearing team gear for the basketball game. At Union, almost everyone would leave the car.

He had to find Alice, but how could he hide himself? Surrounding himself with basketball fans and trying to blend in with them might work.

He leaned over to the guy in the seat beside him. The man was wearing a Deeker jersey. Ben knew Deeker was one of the team's best players, though he didn't follow basketball closely.

"Is it true that Deeker is injured and out tonight?"

That got the attention of the guy beside him, and every fan within hearing distance.

"What? Where did you hear that?"

Ben was vague, but it started a loud and anxious discussion. The train slowed to a halt, and the doors opened. Ben was in the middle of a crowd of worried fans, all asking questions, looking for information on their phones, and Ben was able to keep his head down. The cops were doing their best to check out every traveler, but they were hamstrung by the number of commuters heading home and fighting the basketball fans heading to the arena.

They were looking for a man or woman alone or together, not a pack of basketball fans.

He was able to stay with his new friends until they arrived at the arena. He took a moment in the lobby to check for watchers. Somehow, he had to come up with a plan to find Alice, even though he had no idea where to start.

Things didn't look good.

THIRTEEN

Alice was procrastinating. She needed a plan. She couldn't stay here in the lobby of the arena looking at posters and reading the upcoming team schedules. She prayed for some guidance.

Should she try to find Ben? How would she do that? She could go into the ball game with the tickets she'd been given, but then what? It was dark now, and so, so cold.

"Hey, sis."

Stomach somewhere up in her throat, Alice turned around in shock.

Ben was standing beside her…like a miracle.

"Hey, bro." She wondered if she looked as happy as she felt to be together again. "Want to watch the game?" she asked.

"You got enough money for that?"

There was worry in his gaze. He had no idea she had two free tickets to give them a respite.

She reached into her bag and pulled out the two tickets.

He looked as shocked as she felt.

"You bought tickets?"

She shrugged. "A nice young man gave them to me."

She could see the questions in his gaze, but this wasn't the time.

"Let's go, then." He gripped her elbow and led her toward the entrance. "Where are the seats?"

She passed him a ticket. "You tell me."

"Nosebleed seats."

She was fine with that. "What happened back there? Are you okay? Did he hurt you?" Alice kept her voice low.

"No bones broken, and no bullet holes."

Alice huffed a frustrated breath.

"I'll explain what happened later," Ben replied. "Let's go watch a ball game."

Alice followed his lead toward the elevators to the top floors. They got off on the top level and walked past various vendors until they found the section listed on their tickets.

"Why don't I get us something to drink?" Ben asked. "Can I have some cash?"

Alice dug into her bag and pulled out what was left of their funds, but she wasn't going to let this go. When Ben reached for the money, she shook her head and kept it just beyond his grasp.

"I asked you a question."

Ben kept his hands at his sides, leaving the money with her. "I'll tell you once we're seated. I promise. I want to hear what happened to you, as well."

Alice frowned and passed over the bills.

Once they were seated, drinks in hand, Alice returned to her question. "I want to know what happened back at the mall."

Ben grimaced. "The security guard recognized me."

Alice tried to read his expression. "So much for our disguises. You think he reported you?"

"The disguises won't help with anyone who knows us well. We have some history. He was probably thrilled to find out I'm in trouble and then be the one to turn me in."

Alice knew she should be worried about other enemies Ben might have made, but she was more interested in the connection between the security guard and the person sitting beside her. Something about his expression told her there was a story here. She knew very little about this man she was trusting with her life. He was a good cop, had lived in the city and was resourceful.

She wanted to know more.

"How did you convince him not to turn you in?"

Ben's eyes skittered away from hers. Alice had been a schoolteacher and mother for many years. She understood prevarication and evasion.

"How did you convince him?"

Ben looked down, checked the empty seats beside them and finally capitulated.

"I knocked him out."

Alice's mouth dropped. "You knocked out the security guard? *A security guard?* That's big. People are going to know. Everyone's going to think you've gone rogue."

Ben met her gaze again. "I said I'd keep you safe."

Despite herself, a little ball of warmth uncurled inside her. Ben was keeping his promise. He was placing her safety above his own reputation.

It's his job, she reminded herself.

"You couldn't have just explained things to him? What happened between you two?"

Ben didn't answer right away.

Alice was trusting God and her own feelings when it came to Ben, but she had to be smart here. It wasn't just whether Ben was on the side of the angels. It was also about who he was as a person.

"Ben, I'm trusting you. Are there other people we might run into who will have a problem with you? Did you…do something?"

Ben was torn. He didn't want to expose himself to Alice. To anyone. But he couldn't bear to have her thinking the worst of him.

He needed her to trust him, but he knew it went beyond that, and that was going to be a problem. Still, she should know who he was, know what drove him, since she *was* trusting him.

He shook his head. "No, I didn't *do* anything. Not like you're thinking."

He glanced around their seat section. It was still mostly empty and showed no signs of any trouble.

He sighed. "My first partner when I started on the force was an older guy named Mort."

"Mort," Alice repeated.

"Yeah." Ben allowed a slight smile to touch his lips. "If you'd met him, you'd realize he couldn't have had any other name. He was a lifetime cop, was married to the job, and he was a great partner for a rookie. He had no ambitions to rise through the ranks. He was exactly where he wanted to be, on the streets, helping people. He taught me a lot in the two years we were together."

Alice pressed a hand on his, as if she knew this wasn't going to have a happy ending.

"One thing Mort hated was driving. And I was happy to be behind the wheel. He wasn't the fittest guy, not at his age, but he was smart. Everyone knew him, everyone liked him—at least, if you were on the good guys' side.

"Things were mostly good those two years. Not that everything was pretty."

As a cop, he'd seen things most people didn't. It had taken a while for him to toughen up.

"I learned a lot, got my feet under me in the job and Mort and I worked well together. I had to take leave when Laura, my wife, had cancer. They caught it too late. There was nothing they could do."

"I'm so sorry, Ben," Alice said.

He nodded, acknowledging her comment, but his gaze was still on the people around them.

"While I was on leave, Mort got a new partner, guy named Arnold. He was about my age. That security guard, the one I knocked out, is Arnold's brother. He's a few years older than me. He has an entitled attitude, and Arnold had that same attitude."

"He's a cop? The brother?"

"Was. I heard he retired a couple of years ago."

"So why doesn't he like you?"

"Arnold and Mort were chasing a suspect, Arnold was driving and there was a crash. Driver error. Mort died."

Alice gripped his hand. "And you blame him for Mort's death?"

"No, I blame me."

Ben didn't know why he said that. He didn't tell people about that guilt. It wasn't rational, and Ben was a rational guy.

Alice didn't tell him he wasn't responsible. She didn't say anything. She sat there holding his hand. It was nothing really, but he wanted to relax into that comfort. He wasn't a touchy-feely guy, but right now, her hand on his meant a lot.

When he looked at her face, her eyes were closed. *She's praying,* he thought. He'd seen her like that on and off throughout the day. When they were in a difficult situation, she'd pray.

Ben hadn't prayed for a long time, but the thought that Alice was praying for him was strangely warming.

He cleared his throat. "I know it doesn't make a lot of sense, but Mort always said that a good cop shouldn't have divided loyalties. He'd never married, never had kids. If I'd been with him, the accident wouldn't have happened. I read the reports. I was a better driver than Arnold."

Alice's eyes were open again. "So why would that man want to turn you in? Did you fight with him after the crash?"

"No, but some of the other cops made it clear that they blamed Arnold and thought I would have avoided the accident. At the funeral, Arnold came to talk to me, and I couldn't. I just couldn't, so I walked away from him. I'm not proud of that, but with Mort and Laura both—I wasn't in a good place.

"The guy resigned. I heard he ended up an alcoholic. I know there's not a lot I could've done, but I didn't help. I did try to reach out to him later, after I'd finally gotten myself in a better place, but it was too late, and he wouldn't talk to me.

"I know his brother blames me, and I think he'd like to find some way to make us equal, to have the same flaws."

"Excuse me." A voice came from beside them. Ben looked up and saw a family waiting to get past them to get to their seats.

Ben was relieved to have the discussion interrupted. Alice needed to know that the problem with this one person wasn't likely to cause any more difficulties for them. She didn't need to get any further into his head. Her sympathy was breaking through walls he'd put up that he thought were a lot stronger.

The problem with the guard wasn't over. When Arnold's brother regained consciousness, he was going to tell people that Ben had attacked him and knocked him out.

Some of his fellow officers, the ones involved in Chris's protection, might guess Ben had gone off the grid to protect Alice. Others might think he was the mole, the source of the leak. He was completely on his own. And he was responsible for Alice.

And once again, he'd been distracted by Alice and not noticed the family waiting for them. It could have been someone from the gang there to grab her. It could have been a cop wanting to take them in, to ostensibly protect her and question him. That would put Alice in a vulnerable position.

He couldn't risk her safety like that. He had no one else he trusted to protect her right now, and he had to fight this attraction to her so that he could do his job.

He needed to find a safe place they could spend the night, and not spend their time together getting into his history. He didn't need to make her understand him. He didn't need her praying for him. He didn't need her to hold his hand.

He blew out a breath. He needed this to be over.

Alice slid over so the family could pass them. She smiled perfunctorily. Once the family had moved to the far end of the row, she turned to Ben.

"As soon as that man regains consciousness, he's going to tell them about you."

Ben nodded. "I don't think he saw you. I'm hoping your disguise still works."

Alice drew in a long breath. "Okay, what do we do after the game?"

She had no idea what to do in the city with so little cash, no one she could reach out to, and no credit card or bank resources. They couldn't stay outside. It was going to be cold tonight. She'd seen warnings on the TV screens they'd passed. The city had issued an extreme cold weather alert and were opening more resources for those living on the streets. Maybe they could ask a homeless person for tips about where to go?

Ben scanned their area and then looked down at the basketball court. The building was filling up. The game would be starting soon.

"I've been thinking on this. We can't go to a normal hotel, motel or anyplace that will want to see our ID or a credit card. I know some places that take cash, but we don't have a lot, and some of the people in those places might catch on that I'm a cop. They are also likely to be susceptible to pressure from the gang that's after you."

Alice swallowed. She'd considered this, as well.

"I don't have relatives in the city, and my friends are cops or cop-adjacent," he explained.

"They wouldn't trust you? Believe your story?" she asked. She had only known Ben a day, but she trusted him absolutely. Did he not have friends who would feel the same way?

Ben made another scan of their section. "I want to say yes. There are men I'm tight with. But…"

Alice struggled to understand for a moment. "You don't want to implicate them?"

"I'm convinced there's a mole. Someone trusted who's turned. Their best play is to convince everyone that the mole is me."

Alice could feel her mouth drop open. Ben, the mole? That made no sense.

"But you aren't. You can't be. It's only because of you that I'm not already with those men."

Ben nodded. "But because of me the police don't know where you are. I've isolated you. For all they know, the gang does have you."

"But they don't." Alice was ready to spit in aggravation. "I can tell them…" She trailed off. She couldn't tell them anything, not now. Not until the trial was over or the mole was neutralized.

Ben put a hand on hers. "I know it'll all come out right in the wash. When it's all over, everyone will know I was doing the right thing. And most importantly, you'll be safe. But—"

"But?" She needed to know. She had more at stake here than anyone.

"I'd be putting anyone I called in a tight place. And I don't know what the mole's been disseminating while we've been out of touch."

Alice drew in another long breath. What he said made sense, but she'd been hoping he had a solution. She'd been counting on him to solve their problem.

Noise swelled in the arena. Far below them, the teams were coming out. Alice didn't pay much attention to the announcers, or the anthems. She stood and went through the motions with the people around them.

The opening tip off happened on the court, and Alice tried to look interested, but it was hard to concentrate on a sport that she didn't care about when there was so much going on in her own life.

After what seemed like an eternity but wasn't yet halftime, Alice turned to Ben. "I need to use the restroom."

She could almost see the wheels turning in his head.

"I'm fine on my own. It would look strange if you went with me."

He finally nodded. "Be as quick as you can."

Alice found her way to the women's bathroom. She didn't rush. There was no one else in the room, and it was quiet and felt safe.

It was tempting to stay longer, but she knew Ben would worry. And there was only so much time one could spend here before things looked…odd.

On her way back to their section, a flicker on a

video screen caught her attention. Normally, it would only broadcast sports information, but right now, she was looking at a picture of Ben.

It was grainy, and she suspected it had been taken with a phone camera earlier today, and it was recognizably Ben. Under the picture was a message stating that anyone who saw him should call the police because he was a person of interest in a kidnapping and an assault on a security guard.

Alice's picture followed, but it was still the old photo they'd used earlier today, showing her with her hair long.

But Ben... There was a good chance he'd be recognized.

At halftime, everyone would come out here to get refreshments, use the facilities and stretch their legs. They'd see the photos. This was no longer a safe place.

She wanted to go back and hide in the bathroom. The idea of safety and warmth for a few hours had been so appealing. Now they'd be on the run again, and the temperature outside would be even colder.

Saying a quick prayer for strength, she went back to their seats. She saw Ben's eyes track her as soon as she was in sight. His brows creased, so her expression must have revealed her worry.

"Let's get a hot dog."

Ben was able to read her body language well enough to know something wasn't right. He nodded and led the way out of their section, eyes scanning the area.

As soon as they were clear, he asked, "What's the problem?"

Alice could feel the panic welling up and fought to

keep it down. Ben grabbed her hand and pulled her into an alcove.

"They have a recent picture of you, looking just like you do now. It was on a monitor when I came out of the bathroom. And it'll soon be halftime."

He nodded his comprehension. "We have to leave."

Alice bit her lip.

"You still have some cash?"

She nodded.

"Let's get some team beanies. It might change my appearance just enough, and you're going to need a hat outside."

She refused to whine. Ben was doing everything he could to keep her safe. He'd risked his very reputation with the police force. She could handle a bit of cold.

She got the hats, more expensive than they should be for what they were, and they headed to the elevator.

They were fine until they came out into the lobby. The monitors there were broadcasting Ben's picture.

Before they got very far, someone yelled, "Hey, it's the guy on the TV."

Ben grabbed her hand, and they ran out the arena doors.

FOURTEEN

Once they were out of the arena, Ben led them down a dark side street at a run. They paused while he listened for footsteps behind them, and he pulled one hat over Alice's shorn tresses and the other over his.

The temperature had dropped drastically while they'd been inside, and every breath they took puffed in the night air. They needed shelter. Fast. They also needed to get as far away from the arena as possible. He could hear sirens on the frozen air, headed toward them. No footsteps. But they needed to move.

"Do you still have your pass?"

Alice paused, reached into her bag, felt around and brought her hand out with the pass.

Ben led her up to the main street, two blocks over from where they'd escaped. Once there, they didn't see any police cars nearby, and they were only a couple of buildings from a transit stop. It was a streetcar stop, and one of the streetcars was coming toward them. Alice jogged over, Ben at her heels. The red vehicle stopped, and the doors opened. Alice scanned her pass, and Ben his, and they made their way toward the back of the car. About half the seats were taken, and Ben ushered Alice into one that was available.

They were exposed to anyone looking in from the street, but they were warm and moving away from the arena. That was the best they could do for the moment.

Alice gripped his hand. "How long do the street-cars run?" she asked, trying to smile.

"Long enough for us to come up with another plan, I hope."

Ben checked the car. He hadn't paid much attention to the route marker on it. He'd been more interested in getting out of the cold and away. This was the Queen Street car. Finally, a break. He couldn't have picked a better route.

Queen Street ran east and west from one end of the city to the other. That gave them a long time to sit and think.

Ben ran over the route in his mind. They'd soon head over the Don Valley and be in the east end. There was a long stretch of up-and-coming neighborhoods, and then The Beaches, an upscale area full of bars and restaurants and boutiques. And the yacht clubs. A memory popped up.

After Mort and Laura died, Ben had gotten a new partner. He'd had several over the years, but Ed was the one who came to mind when he thought of yacht clubs.

With no wife, no hobbies and too much time on his hands, Ben had helped Ed with his boat. Ed's old wooden sailboat had been a money and time pit. His partner had provided the money, but Ben had offered his time for a few years until Ed retired. Then Ben got a different partner, and they'd lost touch.

Ben had forgotten most of what he'd learned about

boats due to lack of application. He certainly wouldn't try to sail one now. But he remembered that at the end of each boating season, the boats were hauled out of the water. Lake Ontario would often freeze over, so each fall, the boats were put up on jacks in the yacht club yard.

He'd helped prepare Ed's boat for haul out, and he'd helped work on the boat over the winter. Ed would come down, plug a heater into one of the power sources the club provided and they'd work inside the covered boat. The heater had provided enough warmth for the small contained space, even though it wasn't insulated.

He had no idea if Ed still had a boat down there. Ed would be well into his eighties now, and the boat had been hard work. But at this time of night, no one would be around a yacht club. The yard would be empty of people. If he and Alice could get into the yacht club yard, and find a boat with a heater, they'd have warmth and privacy for the rest of the night.

It wasn't a perfect solution. The boats were stripped down for the off-season, and the club would be locked up. There would be no water, no bathrooms and probably no food or bedding. On the plus side, no one would be looking for them there.

This was the last stopgap measure. By morning, Ben needed to have a plan, something proactive, rather than reactive. If they kept on running, they'd eventually be cornered.

He needed time to rest. They could only last so long without sleep. And he needed time to think, to consider their problem and come up with a solution. For that, he needed quiet and a chance to focus. This idea, crazy as it might be, could provide that.

* * *

Alice gave Ben time and space. He was staring out the window, but she didn't think he really saw the buildings sliding past them. He was thinking, trying to find a way for them, so she stayed quiet.

She stared out the opposite window of the streetcar. The snow was gray and crusty under the streetlights. Holiday decorations were gone, and the view was uninspiring.

The streetcar began to slow. It wasn't a regular stop. She looked forward and saw the lights of another streetcar halted on the tracks in front of them.

Was there a problem on the tracks? One of the quirks of a streetcar was that it could only run on its prescribed track, just like a train. A stalled car in the same lane meant no streetcars could get past. Buses could swerve into different lanes, but not the streetcars.

She checked to see if they were going to be shunted over to a bus and noticed the flashing lights a block ahead. Red and blue.

It might be nothing. But what if it was something? Could they be checking all the streetcars and buses for her?

She swallowed, throat dry.

She nudged Ben with her elbow and nodded forward. She could see expressions racing over his face—confusion, understanding, concern and then determination.

"Ready to run?"

No, not really. Not if she were honest. But she would.

Ben flipped up the edge of her coat and ran a finger over the lining. "Can you take your coat off, turn it inside out, and carry it with you? That color is bright. Once we're off the car, if you put it on with the liner on the outside, we might be able to hide."

The beanies they had on were dark, and so were Ben's jacket and their pants.

She pulled off her coat, reached into a sleeve and pulled the dark lining to the outside. Ben had his gaze focused on the scene in front of them.

"Coat's done."

"We'll have one chance. When they open the front door to let someone on, we can push open this rear door and run when we hit the ground. I'm hoping no one is being as cautious as they should be on a night this cold."

Alice didn't know if that was a reasonable hope, but she prayed—again. That was *her* hope.

The streetcar stopped. She and Ben were waiting at the top of the steps on the rear exit. Ben was behind her, keeping his face hidden from anyone on the outside. She saw two policemen approach the front door. One stopped by the driver's door, the other headed toward the back of the car.

The driver opened the front door.

"Now," Ben said.

She stepped down, pushing against the doors. They opened, and she jumped down. Before she'd taken more than a step, Ben passed her, grabbed her hand and led her back the way they'd come at a run.

She heard voices calling for them to stop, but at the corner, Ben took a left, and they headed down the residential street. Alice depended on his hand to keep her from losing her balance. The cold had frozen any snow into rock-hard ice, just begging for a fall.

Suddenly, he pulled her up a driveway. The drive wasn't well tended and was lumpy with frozen ice and snow. Alice lost her footing and would have landed on the ground except for Ben grabbing her and bringing her close.

They ducked behind an evergreen in the dark. Alice pulled her inside-out coat on over her shivering limbs. Ben nudged her farther into the darkness. She felt twigs poking her, and needles from the tree tugged at her clothing.

Footsteps came down the street.

"No sign of the suspects. Are you sure they came down this street?"

There was a buzz of static from the radio.

"Hey, you there?"

More buzzing.

"What's wrong with this radio?"

There was some cursing, and the footsteps moved away.

Ben's breath tickled her ear as he breathed more than spoke to her. "Let's go."

Alice was tired. They'd been on the run since morning. She realized she still had so many questions, things she hadn't been able to focus on while she was concentrating solely on avoiding the people trying to capture her. Some of the questions might never be answered, but Ben could provide some answers. If she and Ben found a refuge for the night, she was going to ask those questions.

She moved from foot to foot, trying to keep warm. Her breath escaped in white puffs in the cold air. She was grateful for the hat Ben had bought. With shorter hair, her head was more susceptible to the cold. She had her hands jammed into the pockets of the jacket designed more for appearance than warmth.

Next time she went on the run, she was going to buy a more practical jacket. And warmer gloves.

"Can you walk for a while? Are you warm enough?"

She nodded. Moving was warming her up, and if transit was no longer an option, walking was all they had left. She prayed she could walk as far as they needed before she lost all feeling in her fingers.

Ben was frustrated. The police force, the group he'd devoted his life to, was now his biggest handicap. The resources they could provide well outweighed anything the gang could put together, and it was maddening to know these resources were being utilized to help a criminal.

The only bright side to all this was the knowledge that the mole was someone of importance. To have this much manpower in play and all these resources to spend on finding Alice meant that whoever was behind this had clout. And that meant there was a smaller pool of people who it could be.

If they were able to find refuge in one of the boats at the yacht club, he'd use the time to work the puzzle through. The mole had to be caught.

Meanwhile, Alice was gamely keeping pace with him. He'd started to walk faster, and it was keeping him warm, and Alice, too. It was also getting them to their destination sooner.

He hoped this would work, because they couldn't keep walking indefinitely. He hadn't even told Alice his plan.

"So." He waited for her response.

"So." Her voice was a breathy echo, and he slowed his pace slightly.

"I think I know a place we can stay the night."

"Really?" The relief in her voice answered his question as to how much longer she could keep going. Not long.

"We're about a mile from one of the yacht clubs."

He saw the surprise in her raised brows as they passed under a streetlamp.

"Years ago, I had a partner who had a boat down here. I helped him out for a while. He's long retired now, living in Florida for the winters as far as I know, but I remember helping him work on the boat in the off-season. They have the boats out of the water and up on jacks in the boatyard, and they plug them into power when they're working on them. That way they have power tools and light…and most importantly, heat.

"They unplug them all before they leave for the night, and someone checks that out, but everyone will be gone by now. If we can find a boat with a heater and a ladder, we should be warm and safe until morning."

Alice moved her jaw back and forth as she considered.

"Are you sure they won't look for you there?"

"It's been so long since Ed had a boat here, that I don't think any of my friends and contacts could come up with the idea. It won't be hard to find out if someone is there now, and if so, we'll lay low and try something else."

He just had no idea what that something else could be.

FIFTEEN

Alice couldn't remember the last time she'd been this cold and tired. When Ben finally indicated the yacht club was just up ahead, she could have wept for joy.

Except that her tears would have frozen.

They stopped at the edge of a roadway leading to the club, avoiding the streetlights and taking advantage of every bit of darkness. Ben stood back, scanning the area. The trees were bare, except for an occasional evergreen.

Alice couldn't see anything except a chain-link fence with the shadowy shapes of boats behind it. They were like toys, standing over the ground, held up in metal frames. Giant toys. Most were covered with something that hid the details of their contours and made them look like ghostly footballs.

Ben moved to the gate with Alice on his heels. There was a combination pad on the gate to open it.

"You remember the code?" she asked, impressed.

Ben shook his head. "It's been too long. Even if I remembered the code from back then, it would have been changed by now."

Alice's heart fell. She'd begun to believe in this plan.

Ben put his foot in the chain-links, but only the tip of his boot would fit. Did he plan to climb over? Was she supposed to?

She heard his grunt, then he reached down and untied his boots.

"What are you… Should I?" Alice asked, confused.

Ben shook his head. "No, you stay put. I'll climb over, then I can open the gate for you."

"Is there an alarm?"

The corner of his mouth crooked up. "I hope not."

Alice bit her lip. "No, they count on keeping out intruders with this combination lock. Most of the boats are locked up, and the smaller and more valuable things will have been locked away. Theft and vandalism aren't a big problem."

He shoved his toes in the chain and start climbing.

She could only imagine how cold his feet must be and prayed he wouldn't fall. He reached the top, swung his leg over and dropped to the ground on the other side. Alice hastily picked up his boots and waited at the gate. He moved back, waved his arms, and as promised, the gate opened so she could walk through. No alarms sounded; no lights lit up.

"It wouldn't be a silent alarm, would it?"

Ben shook his head again. "An intruder would be gone before the alarm got to the club members. Some of them don't even live in Toronto. This isn't the place where the big and expensive boats are. This is a blue-collar type of club. At least, it was last time I was here, and it doesn't look like it's changed much."

Ben laced his boots back on with commendable speed, and they walked farther into the club grounds.

The boats were suspended over Alice's head. She heard a tarp flap and flinched, expecting to see some-one there, ready to report them. Or someone with a gun ready to take her from Ben. When nothing happened, and Ben appeared unfazed, she moved forward again. She followed him past the floating shapes, all much bigger up close than she had expected. And these were the smaller ones?

With a grunt, Ben reached under one boat, pulled out a ladder and walked around the boat with it while Alice waited. She kept her feet moving in place, hop-ing to generate some heat.

"The opening in the tarp is over here." He went to the back of the boat and propped the ladder against it. He climbed up while Alice shivered below him, hold-ing the ladder to try to feel useful.

He fumbled with the tarp, muttering, and then pushed into the opening he'd made.

"Just a minute while I check for a heater."

Alice waited. She couldn't feel her toes, and her fingers were difficult to move. A heater sounded like bliss. She was losing herself in a dream of warmth when she heard a noise above her.

Ben reappeared and started to climb down. "No joy."

Alice swallowed a protest. Wouldn't being out of the wind at least be a help? He rubbed his hands together and put the ladder back under the boat.

"No need to advertise our presence."

Alice could hear the tremor in his voice. He was freezing, as well.

Ben checked out a couple more boats and then pulled out another ladder. Again, he circled the boat and found an opening near the back on one side. He propped up the ladder and climbed while Alice prayed for a heater. Was it wrong to ask for God's help when they were breaking in? They could offer restitution, if they just made it through the night.

"Yes!" Alice could hear the relief in Ben's voice. He came down, seeming lighter on the rungs, and then crawled under the boat. He reappeared with an extension cord and attached it to one dangling from the side of the boat under the fitted cover.

"Wait for just a moment. I'm going to plug it in."

It was a long moment in a day full of them. Alice could see his dark shape moving around the boats, and then he was coming back.

"You first." Ben waited at the bottom of the ladder, standing aside to give her the chance to climb. Alice forced her cold hands to grip the rungs and slid her feet forward until her heels caught, to ensure her numb toes didn't slip and drop her to the ground again.

There were metal rails at the top, bordering the outside edge of the boat, and she slid awkwardly between them. Ben was right behind her. She stood up cautiously, head brushing against a frame holding up the cover. She found herself in a narrow cockpit. There was a wheel beside her and narrow seats. It was still cold here, but the wind pushing on the canvas cover thwarted it enough to provide some relief.

Alice slipped aside and let Ben lead the way to a wooden doorway. He opened it and revealed a tiny space with steps leading into a dark hole. She followed him down, moving carefully until she was on a solid floor. She stayed still, unsure what was around her and where she could go.

Ben fumbled around, and then a red light came on, and a little black box on the floor began to blow air. There was a glimmer of illumination from the box, enough to reveal the wooden slats covering the floor in front of the heater.

"Gloves and boots off," Ben ordered. Alice wanted to argue, but as a trickle of warmth flowed out of the precious box, she followed his lead. They sat on the wooden floor, side by side, stiffly working frozen limbs in front of the heat.

Her toes hurt as blood began flowing through them again. Even though they could still see their breath puffing in the air, she could feel the temperature slowly climbing as it warmed around her frozen cheeks.

She doubted it would get very warm in here. This was an epically cold night, and the heater was merely warm. But at least they weren't getting colder, and she felt safe, wrapped in this dark little cocoon.

Ben lifted his eyes to hers. "This feels better."

Alice nodded. With her body starting to warm up, other concerns came to mind. "No one will notice?"

Ben shrugged. "I can't imagine any reason someone would come down to check on their boat at this time of night. Still, I'll see if I can pull up the ladder. If someone does check, they'd just think this boat owner forgot to unplug his boat. They'll unplug the other end of the extension cord, and when they go away again, I'll plug it back in. As long as we're quiet, we should be good until morning."

That sounded amazing to Alice.

Ben climbed the steps to the cockpit and disappeared. Alice heard movement and a couple of grunts, and then he returned.

"The ladder is up, so let's see what else we can find."

Alice remained huddled around the heater while Ben felt his way through the dark space. Behind her back, near her shoulder blades, Alice could feel a cushion on a wooden shelf, as if she was sitting on the floor with a seat behind her.

Suddenly a beam of light blinded her. A flashlight.

"Sorry." Ben pointed the light past her.

Alice could see their hideaway now. There *was* a seat behind her, and one across from it. The seat backs ran along the sides of the boat. There was a door toward the front of the boat, opposite the steps they'd entered by, and a little kitchenette by the steps. It was a tiny house suspended in the air.

Ben went through the forward door and returned smiling with blankets and pillows. "Welcome to the Ritz!"

It was difficult to express how relieved Ben felt.

They were safe, relatively warm, and with the pillows and blankets, they could sleep. The bedding had a musty smell, but that wasn't enough to deter him.

With the tarp over the boat, no one would see their flashlight. There was no one around the yacht club. No one had any reason to look here for them. For the first time in hours, Ben could let some of the tension escape his body and try to think about a solution to their problem instead of constantly watching for a threat.

He wouldn't let down his guard, but he could relax it a bit.

Alice sighed as she snuggled into the blanket.

"To think, this morning my biggest worry was how much work it was going to be to clean out the house."

"I'm sorry." She didn't deserve to have something like this happen to her. Neither did her son.

Alice shook her head. "No need to apologize. It isn't your fault. But I would like to ask you some questions."

Alice had been incredibly trusting throughout this whole nightmare of a day. Ben thought she was over-due for some answers. He nodded, wondering what she was most interested in knowing.

"What exactly did Chris witness? You said it was a murder. But he wouldn't need to be in witness protection if there wasn't something special about it."

Yes, the event that started it all.

"The case is very high profile. The guy murdered was one of the top-ranking gang members in the most violent gang in the city right now."

Her eyes widened.

"Not an ordinary crime of passion, or greed, or a drive-by shooting. It was an execution carried out by a particular member high enough up the hierarchy that he doesn't normally get his hands dirty."

Alice nodded, biting her lip again.

"How did Chris end up seeing it?"

"He'd had a late shift in the lab. Apparently, there's only so much time available for some of their fancy machines, and he'd been slotted in late at night. He was walking home and just happened to be in the wrong place at the wrong time."

"Did they see him when it happened?"

Ben shook his head. "He was smart enough to figure out what was going on and hid. He called 911 and then someone called Sergeant Jones."

Alice nodded. "His godfather."

"Yeah, because Chris is a cop's kid and knew Jones was in homicide, he called him right away. Jones was on duty, figured out what was going on and got Chris away before anyone knew who he was."

"That's when the Antarctic expedition came up?" He could see the wry expression on her face in the low light.

"I wasn't involved with any of that, but with his biology major, it was a good cover. Chris came up with the idea himself."

"That sounds like him. And it worked. I didn't question it for a minute."

Ben let Alice consider what he'd told her.

She drew a breath. "Okay, so he's been temporarily *in the Antarctic* until the trial. What happens after? Does he have to go into hiding for the rest of his life? Can I go with him?"

Ben had wondered if she'd realized the long-term consequences of Chris's testimony. Chris might have to disappear for years, maybe forever. Ben didn't have the answer to Alice's question. There were a lot of variables in play. He didn't want Alice to disappear. He liked her. He liked her more than he should.

It had been an incredibly difficult day, and she had yet to complain. He knew she must have been freezing at various points of the day, and she had every reason to be frustrated with the lack of any plan. Nothing had gone right, unless you counted the fact they'd found a place to hide in a cold boat for the night.

To do his job the way he should, he couldn't let someone distract him. He'd seen the problems that could cause. And aside from the fact that he was currently protecting Alice, which made her his job, thinking about an after didn't help him. Alice hadn't shown any interest in him.

He'd made his decision a long time ago. He'd chosen his job, and that was his top priority. He needed to ignore how he felt about Alice, get her back to her life and then return to his. No distractions.

He should let Alice know what her life was likely to be like, assuming they got through this. He knew he wouldn't factor into it.

"Permanent witness protection was considered when Chris first agreed to testify. He agreed to be isolated until the trial and then go into WP on a permanent basis if necessary. I don't know how you played into that. When the defense lawyers understood we have a strong witness, the idea of a deal was brought up. We're hoping the defendant will help bring down the gang.

"The guy charged is determined not to spend hard time. The man he killed has a lot of friends on the inside who'd like to harm him. The offer to turn wasn't a surprise.

"I know he expected the gang to get him off somehow. But there's been some internal division, thanks to him offing another high-level member. It appeared like this deal would save his butt, save the province a trial and potentially bring down one of the worst gangs we're dealing with in Toronto.

"Then, a couple of months ago, this guy got difficult. He started to nitpick the agreement. He didn't say he wouldn't testify, but he's been complaining about the terms and keeping the lawyers busy negotiating."

Alice watched Ben intently by the fading glow of the flashlight, and he noticed her shiver. He lifted his arm without thought, offering to share warmth. Alice slid under his arm, and he held her against him.

"Now, we good guys aren't idiots. We knew something was up. When your supervisor was up for maternity leave, I was brought into the mix and sent out to keep an eye on you, just in case.

"The deal to testify against his own allies was being fine-tuned, and the trial date was coming up fast. When I heard about the invasion in your home, I knew something was very wrong."

"The mole," Alice said from under his arm.

"Yeah. It's gotta be someone in homicide who didn't know where Chris was until they brought him out to testify, or someone in witness protection who didn't want to tip his hand and waited until Chris was brought out."

"And you think it's someone high up, don't you?"

Ben sighed. "It would be nice to think it was some constable who maybe accidently said too much to the wrong person, but it's more than that. It was one thing when they got to Chris. Another when someone came to your house. Then someone let the gang know when you were being picked up at the hospital. There especially wasn't a lot of time for a warning about that last one. This is someone with access to all the information.

"The media reports coming out now implying I'm the criminal are coming from someone with clout."

Alice looked worried, and he wanted to erase that worry for her. But he wouldn't lie. Like she'd said way back at the start of all this, if she knew what she was up against, she'd be better prepared, and that would hopefully help keep her safe.

"So, what's our plan now?"

Ben leaned back against the seat, tucking the blanket around Alice's shoulders.

"The first and most important thing is keep you safe."

"And Chris." She curled into his side, and it felt good. He'd never had this much trouble keeping his emotions separate from his job.

"Chris is out of my hands," he said. "But you aren't."

SIXTEEN

She shouldn't feel so warm inside at hearing those words. He just meant that she was his responsibility. But as much as she'd enjoyed her independence since she'd been widowed, she enjoyed the sense of comradery she had with Ben, which was ridiculous for so many reasons. She wasn't his teammate. She wasn't his partner. She was his job. And he was good at his job, just like Henry had been. And that meant that his job was his top priority.

That was good for the community at large. It wasn't as good for a woman who might want to be a priority in his life. She needed to remember that, especially since they had a city full of people trying to find them. It was no time to get distracted.

She needed to focus on their problem.

"We need to get the mole to show him or herself. Right?"

Ben stared ahead, though there was little to see in the dim light of the flashlight.

"So we need to figure out what they want badly enough to risk exposing themselves."

Ben's gaze shot to hers, and he started to shake his head.

Alice pressed her palm to his cheek, scratchy with stubble, to stop the negative movement.

"Me. Right now, I'm the only thing we know that they need."

Ben's lips flattened. "Using you as bait is the opposite of keeping you safe."

Alice didn't want to be bait. She wasn't stupid. She didn't want to risk her security. But she also didn't want to be on the run for who knew how long, and she didn't want Chris to have to choose between his principles and her safety or life. She also didn't want Ben to lose the career he obviously loved so much.

"You're sure the mole is in one of two departments. We send one location to homicide, and one to WP, and then we see who shows up with the gang instead of the cops."

She didn't let fear weaken her voice. Ben was watching her, and she wanted to be brave. Still, he shook his head, either because he could sense her fear or for another reason...

"It's an idea, but I'm not going to let you sit there exposed, and there's no way the mole will show up if you're not there." He held up a hand when she tried to speak. "If the first location brings out the cops, they might corner us and put you in the system and in danger again. Then there'll be no chance to lure out the mole to the second location."

Alice didn't want to concede. She wanted a plan, and she wanted this over.

"Then what we need is to get both departments to

a place that's got two sections. Somewhere we can watch both sections at the same time. And if I'm in the middle, between the two, the mole will see me and come out with the gang while the cops are right there to protect me. Once the mole is neutralized, I'll be safe in the system."

Ben frowned, shook his head and sighed. "That makes some sense, even though I hate to admit it. The problem is, where is this place?

"Both sides will want to get there early to stake it out, so we have to be able to arrive without them seeing us and grabbing you before we get into position. It has to have two discrete sections, and somehow, a way for you to be in both places without one side being aware of the other. And I'd like to have some exits, in case this all goes south."

Alice lost her moment of pride. The idea might be good, but she had no clue how to execute it. It needed a very specific location, and she didn't know Toronto well enough. She was a small-town woman in the big city, and she was out of her depth.

Ben watched her and then pulled her head into his shoulder. "I'm sorry, I didn't mean to rain on your parade. I just won't gamble with your safety. But we can sleep on it. I get some of my best ideas while I'm sleeping."

Alice chuckled against his chest, happy they weren't on the outs. "I'm not sure you're going to get a good night's sleep tonight to come up with any eureka moments."

"This isn't quite the five-star experience you're used to?"

"I'm not used to five-star, so you don't need to worry that I'm going to be like a princess complaining about a pea under my mattress. I'm warm now, and my body is tired enough to drop off, but my mind is buzzing, so it's hard to imagine drifting off to a relaxing sleep right now."

Ben's arm tightened around her. "It's not a relaxing situation. But you can rest. We might as well turn off this flashlight to save some battery. I'll keep watch."

Alice knew Ben was bearing all this weight on his own shoulders. She didn't think he trusted in God like she could. Although she'd been cold and afraid and still had no idea what the next day would bring, her faith was her bedrock. She wanted to ease some of Ben's burden, but she didn't want to come across as preachy.

"Ben, I want to thank you for all you've done today, but I also want you know I'm not putting all this on you."

She felt his shoulder stiffen underneath her cheek, and his arm tense around her shoulders. She ignored that and kept on.

"I believe that God is the one in ultimate control, and I trust that He's using you to take care of me. In the end, everything is in His hands, not yours. I don't know if you're a believer, but I want you to know that I don't believe we're alone."

Alice waited out the silence.

"I haven't had much of a relationship with God for a long time, Alice," Ben finally responded. "You don't find what happened today to be a challenge to what you believe?"

Alice was relieved he didn't mock her or put down

her faith. She hoped whatever relationship he'd had with God in the past could be revived, and she was happy to share what to her were signs of her Father watching over them.

"We're safe here. Chris, as far as we know, is safe, as well. And even though people have been hurt, no one has died. Every time we've been in trouble, something has happened to help us, and we're still here. Sometimes it was an idea we had, and sometimes it seemed like luck, but I know it was God."

She felt the tension in Ben's body relax. "It would be nice to think that if I mess up, you'll still have someone taking care of you."

"I feel the same way, Ben. I believe that God is taking care of you, as well."

Ben sighed. "I stopped thinking like that after Laura and Mort."

Ben preferred to leave the past in the past. He didn't understand why he was talking to Alice about this.

She was facing an uncertain tomorrow, and he was feeling the pressure of taking care of her. She must have picked up on that and was trying to relieve that stress.

He liked Alice. A lot. And he respected her. It was easy talking to her while they lay in the dark, huddled together for warmth.

"Your first partner and your wife," Alice spoke into the dark.

Ben nodded. He knew Alice couldn't see him, but they were close enough that he knew she'd feel his gesture.

"Laura died a week after Mort."

He felt more than heard her gasp.

"It was a difficult time. I felt guilty for abandoning Mort. But Laura needed me, as well. And I felt guilty for resenting her illness and how it impacted my job. I'm not good in that kind of crisis. Give me someone who's broken a law, hurt someone, and I'll go after them. But cancer? I can't go after that. I couldn't do anything to protect her from that. I couldn't make her feel better. I was helpless and frustrated.

"I knew I could do something if I was working, but sitting at the hospice was so…passive. As much as I tried not to, I resented that."

Alice gripped his arm, offering comfort.

"After Laura…died, I was determined to focus on work and not get involved with anyone again."

"There hasn't been anyone since?" Her voice was concerned, not prying.

He shook his head, and his chin brushed the top of her head.

"Do you not get lonely?"

Did he? He had his cop family, the men he worked with. They had common goals, and they trusted each other. Ben usually volunteered to work holidays so the family guys could spend time at home. When he wasn't working, there were other single cops he could hang out with. Sometimes going home alone at the end of a difficult shift wasn't great, but he knew it was better than the alternative.

"When I got back to work after Mort's and Laura's funerals, I was paired up with someone new. Not Ed the boat guy. He was next. My second partner was a young guy about my age. His fiancée was another cop he'd met on the job."

Ben remembered the guy discussing this all very seriously. He'd almost made Ben think it could work.

"He and I were called in to a robbery. His fiancée and her partner were first on the scene.

"It was an armed robbery of a pawn shop. She was hit in the arm, but it was just a graze. Her partner was chasing the suspect while I called for reinforcements. My guy wouldn't leave her, even when she told him to go help her partner.

"I gave chase once I'd made the call, but by then, it was too late. Her partner took a bullet in the lungs. He didn't make it."

Once again, he felt Alice gasp.

"You have to have a clear head in this job. It's better not to have a pressure point, a lever that can trip you into making a mistake, because a mistake can cost lives. So it might be lonely sometimes, but it's better than carrying around a load of guilt. It's better than failing and someone ending up dead."

He didn't look at Alice, grateful that it was dark. He didn't want to see her face. He probably shouldn't have shared that story. He didn't normally tell anyone. Only a handful of people knew it.

The young woman who'd been shot in the arm had felt the loss of her partner deeply, and despite all the planning and talking, the two of them broke up. Both of them left the force less than a year later. It was a sad, messy situation all around.

There *was* a reason he'd shared the story, he realized. Ben needed Alice to know just who he was and what he had to offer. And even more than that, Ben had needed the reminder. He was feeling too much for Alice. How could he protect her if his mind wasn't clear? He needed to be objective enough to make the right decisions.

What if Alice were shot in the arm, and he had the choice of staying with her or catching the mole?

Instinctively, he knew he would want to protect her in the hypothetical situation. He couldn't put the greater good at risk. The needs of the many…that was what he'd dedicated himself to.

The quiet stretched out. "I guess that's what it was with Henry," she eventually said.

"Your husband?"

"My husband was a good cop. He really was. But he wasn't as good at being a husband and father. I guess he had to make that same choice."

Ben felt his anger rise, but it didn't make sense. Why should he be upset that the man had been a good cop?

"Thanks for sharing that with me. I've always resented that his job came first. He missed birthdays, holidays… The job was his top priority. I'm not going to say cops shouldn't marry, but I guess some shouldn't." Alice pulled in a long breath. "I promised myself I'd never get involved with another police officer. I can understand what you're saying about the job being important, and I agree. But I took second place for twenty-five years so that Henry could be a good cop. If I ever find someone else, I want to be top priority for once."

Ben opened his mouth, wanting to dispute that. He wasn't saying every cop had to sacrifice his or her personal life. Or was he?

A family, a relationship was more than birthday parties. Sometimes it was cancer and waiting at a hospice.

What Alice said made sense. She deserved someone who would show her how exceptional she was, not someone who put his job first and made her feel second best. That meant she could never be with someone like him.

He'd been telling himself the same thing all day, so there was no good reason for him to feel like he'd been sucker punched.

Alice was his job. That's all.

SEVENTEEN

Alice felt Ben's jaw clench where it rested on her head. It wasn't difficult to figure out that what she'd said had upset him.

She hadn't wanted to offend him, but she'd needed to remind herself, as well as him, that they were looking for completely different things from their futures.

She pulled away from him slightly. "Would it be okay for me to look around a bit?"

"You want to see what the boat is like? Or is there something you need?"

She wanted space, but that wasn't all. "I just want to see what's here. Maybe there's something we can use. And I'd like to find out who this boat belongs to, so I can thank them later. And reimburse them, if needed."

Ben passed her the flashlight, and she stood. It was colder without the shared body heat, but moving around should help. She'd moved around more today than she had in years.

She didn't see her breath now, thanks to the little heater that was spreading warmth throughout the cabin. There were sliders along the back of the bench seats, so she started there. They were mostly empty, but she found a can of beans.

"I found food!" She passed the can to Ben.

He took it and blew some dust off. "Maybe you can find a can opener? And utensils?"

Alice shrugged and kept looking. The boat had been emptied of a lot, but she found a drawer with flatware and, joy of joys, a can opener. She passed that to Ben with a smirk. While he worked on that, she moved forward to where there was a narrow bathroom.

"Is there any chance this works?" Having a bathroom, and maybe even water…

"Not in these temps."

She turned the tap, but nothing happened.

There was a closet across from the bathroom, and there she hit the jackpot. There were some old jackets, hats and scarves. They smelled of diesel and damp, but she grabbed them and brought them back to Ben.

He had the can of beans open and was waiting for her with two forks.

He raised his eyebrows. "That's a score."

Alice passed the garments over.

"I'm surprised they left anything fabric behind where it's likely to mold." He lifted and examined the items as he spoke.

"Maybe they use the clothes when they work on the boat. I don't care why the stuff is here, but I'm happy it is."

Ben nodded in agreement. "When we leave in the morning, it can help us change up how we look."

"Exactly." They didn't mention what they'd be

doing, or where they'd be going in the morning, but it seemed they both agreed they'd need to move on.

"Ready for fine dining?"

Alice shook her head. "Can I look around a little more? I'd really like to find out who our benefactor is."

Ben waved a hand, indicating she should continue. "Any paperwork would probably be in the nav table." He pointed at a desk-like space near the stairs they'd descended.

Alice slid in onto the seat and found that the table raised. Sure enough, there was paper, pens, charts and things she didn't recognize under the table. She ripped a corner off one of the pieces of paper, picked up a pen, and searched through the paperwork in the light of the fading flashlight.

"There are a few different receipts made out to a Peter Dawson. That's probably him, right?"

"If not, he should know who the owner is."

"Okay, I'm writing down that name and the address they use—it's on Greenwood, which sounds familiar for some reason."

"It's one of the subway stops."

Alice frowned. "I don't remember where that one is."

"It's on the east–west line, not too far from here."

She folded up the paper and put it in her bag, hoping she'd be able to thank Peter Dawson one day soon. Just having a space to feel safe for a few hours was a blessing. Her attitude, which had been nosediving, took a tick upward.

She came back to sit down with Ben, and they shared the beans. They were cold and not very appealing, but they were food, and she didn't know when they'd be able to eat again. She had a feeling that once they left this boat, they'd be exposed and on the run once more.

Despite the heater, she was feeling the chill again. She shivered, and Ben held up his arm.

"Come on, we need to huddle up for what's left of this night. I'll try to brainstorm a plan if I can. Even if we don't sleep, we can relax and let our bodies rest."

He was right. And even if she feared she was enjoying his company more than she should, for now they had this strange time together. She'd just have to deal with any messy feelings later.

She remembered how she'd told Ben she was trusting God to watch over them. She needed to take that to heart for more than just this frantic game of hide-and-seek with the gang. God had brought Ben into her life in time to protect her. He would protect her heart as well, wouldn't He?

She slid back under Ben's arm, and he wrapped the blanket around them. He passed her a scarf from the clothing she'd found, and she wrapped it around her neck, and then relaxed against him. She could feel the strong beat of his heart under her ear. She hadn't experienced the closeness and comfort of another human body for a long time, and it felt good.

For tonight, she decided to stop worrying about tomorrow and the future that would come after that. She would rest and use the time to prepare for whatever came next. Anything else she'd leave up to her heavenly Father. She drifted off to the steady breathing of the man beside her.

* * *

Ben felt Alice's breathing deepen and her body relax against his. He repositioned himself as she sank into sleep. His mind was too busy for him to follow her.

They'd survived today, which was a miracle. He started to list everything that had occurred to keep her safe against all odds. First, she'd had that hidey-hole in her home, and she'd had her phone with her to call for help. At that point, no one had realized the danger she was in, not until Toronto had informed him of the attack on her son.

The thugs running the police car off the road had certainly indicated their high level of desperation. Ben had gotten her to the hospital unharmed, and then he'd almost lost her again.

He had to remind himself that she wasn't his to lose.

As he ran through the day in his head—the mall, the haircuts, the underground PATH, the ball game and now the boat—he could almost believe that her God had watched over them. Her God. At one time, he'd claimed God as his, too, but he'd let that slide. After Mort and Laura died, he'd shut out a lot of things.

Well, if God was out there, He needed to find them a way to expose the mole. They couldn't keep running like this, not with the police and the gang both after them. Ben was running out of resources. He couldn't tell Alice, since she was depending on him, but the net was closing in around them.

Come daytime, people would arrive at the yacht club, and they might be found. Although they could use the coats and scarves Alice had found to change up their appearance a bit, they couldn't stay outside. It was too cold, and they didn't have much money left to move around, feed themselves or provide shelter.

He shifted, bringing Alice closer, keeping her warm under their blankets. It was hard to imagine that they hadn't known each other twenty-four hours ago. Now, she trusted him with her life. He'd warned her of the danger she was in to keep her alert, but he hadn't pressed it. He had no illusions, however, that if the gang got her, no one would see her again.

His body was gradually unwinding, fatigue from the day setting in. He reached around Alice and set an alarm on his watch. If he did fall asleep, they needed to be up and out of here before daylight, when someone could find them. Thankfully, he always wore a watch, since they were keeping their phones off. He was also thankful that daylight started late this far north at this time of year.

He shifted, trying to get as comfortable as he could. He didn't need to encourage a cramp, which might wake Alice up. He couldn't see her since they'd turned off the flashlight again to conserve what little battery was left, but he could feel her lying warm and trusting on his chest.

Alice had been so strong and smart throughout this difficult day they'd had. Henry had been a lucky man. Alice said she didn't come into the city much, so even if they made it through the next few days and she didn't end up in witness protection somewhere, he was unlikely to see her again once this was over. She didn't even know the subway stops, east and west of downtown. Subway stops…

His mind was wandering, sleep catching at the edge of his consciousness, but suddenly a light switched on in his head.

Subway stops. They needed a place with exits, where they would have two different locations they could watch at the same time. Greenwood was of no value for that. It was an ordinary underground subway stop.

There were subway stops where the different lines crossed and the platforms for the different lines were on separate levels. But you couldn't see both trains from any place at the same time, and they couldn't each watch one and communicate since their phones had to remain off.

But there were aboveground subway stations. They weren't the contained spaces the underground ones were. In fact, there were stations on the north–south line that had a walkway crossing over the tracks from the north side to the south side. They'd passed through some of those stops on their way to the hospital. He'd been extra alert because there was so much open space and places where people could appear and disappear.

The haze of sleep faded as his mind started to race. He could tell one department Alice was coming on the north train at a specific time and tell the other that she was coming on the south train. He could watch from the walkway overhead and see which side didn't come with cops. Then he'd know which department contained the leak. If they were lucky, the mole might even show up.

He worked through the details in his head, and it made sense. This could work. Alice didn't need to be there. He could find some safe place for her and then deal with this on his own. With the leak contained to one department, he could work with the other one.

If he set it up early, it could be settled before Chris needed to testify. That would be a stroke of luck. Well, Alice wouldn't call it luck. She'd call it an answer to prayer. And he might as well, too, if they could pull this off.

He glanced at the glowing dial on his watch. He could still get a few hours of sleep, and he needed to if he was going to perform well tomorrow. He did his best to set aside the plan whirring through his mind and instead focus on Alice.

Her head rested on his shoulder, her hair, now short and wispy, tickling under his chin and tangling with the stubble that was growing in since his shave. He allowed himself the luxury of running his hand down her arm and back up, bringing her a little closer to him, warming him, inside and out.

For tonight, he could enjoy being her protector. After tomorrow, he might never see her again, but he would treasure tonight. Even with the air cool enough to make his nose cold and the hard floor under him, he thought this might just be the most enjoyable night he'd had in a long time.

EIGHTEEN

Alice woke to the sound of beeping in her ear. It took a moment to place where she was.

Her nose was cold. Very cold. And her bottom was numb on a hard surface. The rest of her was warm, and she was wrapped around another person.

A male person. Not Henry, who was the only man she'd ever been this close to before. She wondered if she was dreaming, and then the events of the previous day crashed to the front of her mind.

She tensed and glanced up. She couldn't see Ben in the dark, but he relaxed his arm around her, allowing her to sit upright. The cold immediately overcame the lingering warmth of his body. She flushed, self-conscious.

"Good morning." She forced the words out through her tired throat, and her voice came out raspy.

"Let's hope so. How did you sleep?" His voice was roughened, too.

She checked her fingers and toes for feeling. Her neck was slightly sore from being bent against him while she slept.

"No bones broken, no bullet holes. I think I might have to dispute the five-star rating, but honestly, I slept surprisingly well. Thank you, Ben."

She didn't know if he'd managed to get any sleep, but he'd made it possible for her to do so, and she was grateful. She hoped he hadn't done so at the expense of his own rest. It wasn't a completely altruistic concern. She was depending on him.

Of course, she was more invested in his well-being than just as her protector. She was afraid she was starting to care for him. A lot.

"You're welcome. I slept better than expected as well."

"Really?" She couldn't disguise the skepticism in her tone.

She was close enough to feel his nod. "I may have come up with a plan. One to expose the mole and end this ordeal."

She was glad that he had a solution, but for some reason, it hurt to hear him call what they'd been through an ordeal. Realistically, yes, it had been an ordeal for her, too, but she hadn't hated it all. It had been the most exciting thing that had happened to her in years, maybe ever. Between bouts of paralyzing panic and freezing cold, she'd felt alive and vital in a way she hadn't since Henry died.

She cleared her throat. "Sounds good. What do we need to do?" She felt him stiffen in response to her words.

"Alice, you've been incredible through all of this, but I don't think I need you to be part of what I'm planning."

Her first reaction was sadness. Then disappointment. Then came anger. She had been part of all of this, and while she might not have saved the day, she'd helped. She'd had some good ideas. Now he was just going to set her aside?

Yes, he was just like Henry. And right now, that was *not* a compliment.

"Then what am I supposed to do? Stay hiding here on the boat?" She knew she sounded angry, and she didn't care. She was angry.

His sigh was rich with frustration.

"I need to find a safe place for you while this all goes down, but, no, you can't stay here on the boat. We should be out of here by daylight. That's why I set my alarm."

Alice pushed away, ignoring the cold air that filled the warm space between them.

"What's *your* plan?"

"It's your plan, the idea you brought up. I just worked out the location."

She appreciated hearing that *her* plan was good, but she still was upset that he didn't want her to be part of it.

"What location?"

"Rosedale."

"Rosedale," she repeated. Where had she come across that name lately? Wait. The subway stop. She tried to picture it, but she'd never done more than pass through there.

"You mean the subway station, right? I don't know that one. Why do you think it will work well for what you have planned?"

"Let's start to clean up while I explain." Ben turned

on the flashlight, which was marginally brighter than she remembered it being last night.

Alice pulled the blanket off her shoulders and shivered in the cold.

"First, it's an aboveground station, so there are more exits and more visibility."

He placed the empty can of beans in the kitchen sink, while Alice folded up the blankets.

"It also has a walkway over the tracks that connects the north and southbound trains."

Alice nodded. "So there's the north platform and the south platform, which offers two separate areas, but—" she swallowed the *we* she'd almost voiced "—you can watch both sides at once."

"Exactly. I'll call each department and tell them that you're coming to claim their protection. I'll let them know you're arriving on the subway. Since the trains run so frequently, they won't know which one you're on. We'll tell them you plan to get off earlier if anything looks off on your way to Rosedale or if you think anyone is checking the trains before that station. Since you've been attacked, you're nervous and will only do this if everything works out the way you call it.

"If one department thinks you're arriving on the south train at the same time as the other thinks you're coming north, I can be on the walkway and see where the cops show up, and where someone else does."

She could picture it in her mind now. It looked perfect for what they—no, what he wanted.

"Would the mole not just send cops, anyway? Others in whatever department he's in will probably hear about this. You can't be sure your call will get through to him and only him."

"It's possible there will be cops on both sides, but time is getting short. The trial starts today. He could send the cops, but he'll also need to get you away from them immediately. I think he's going to have to be there to make sure nothing goes wrong. We're not going to give him time to make a lot of backup plans."

She wanted to nitpick his proposal, but Ben had given it a lot of thought.

"So, the cops show up on one side, and cops and gang members and hopefully the mole on the other. Then what?"

"Then I'll know which side I can trust and tell them where you are."

Alice placed a carefully folded blanket on the bench seat.

"And where is this safe place you're going to stash me? This boat is the only truly safe idea we've had since we left my house yesterday, and you said it's not going to work once it's daylight."

"A library. Or a coffee shop someplace not too far away but where no one will be looking for you."

Alice spread her hands. "If those are the first places you think of, isn't that where any smart cop will also look? Won't they be checking out the area after you call in? And what if there are cops on both sides of the platform and they spot you and come after you before you figure out where the gang and the mole are?"

Ben frowned at her. "I can keep my mouth shut. You call the number you have to connect to the guys with Chris."

Alice crossed her arms, thinking of the potential problems with Ben's plan to keep her *stashed* someplace.

"What if the mole doesn't show up? How will we find out if he's in homicide or witness protection? Even if I get through to Chris, he might need to testify for more than one day. Where do I stay then? If I call from my phone, they can track me. How do I know if someone shows up that they're safe?"

Ben blew a breath out through his mouth, which fogged in the cold. His lips were narrow and tense.

"It's not a perfect plan, I know. But it's the best we've come up with. And there's a pretty good chance I can slip away and get back to you. Then we can make the call to let Chris know you are safe so he can go testify. We'll tell Chris's team that they have to watch you as well."

Alice looked directly at Ben. "And what if the mole sees you before you see him? Won't he also just slip away if he doesn't see me, as well?"

Ben's gaze moved to the low ceiling over their heads. His jaw clenched.

"That's a risk. A *slight* risk."

Alice pressed her advantage. "If the cops think I'm looking for them, they will wait on the platform, right? So that I would know to go to them. But if the mole sends someone or comes himself, he's not going to stand on the platform with a bunch of officers for long, is he? He's going to need to see me, isn't he? Otherwise, he can stay hidden until I show up. And if I don't, he vanishes. Then, poof! We're back to square one."

Ben crossed his own arms. "You can't be on both

of the trains at the same time, so that can't be helped whether you're there or not."

"But if we see the cops, the real cops on one side, I can go down to the other side. I can keep a good distance back, but that might bring whoever it is out of hiding."

"Alice, I don't want you to be bait, not in person, not where there's a real risk."

Alice drew in a breath. "I've been in danger since yesterday morning. And I'm not afraid."

She held up a hand when Ben wanted to interrupt.

"I'm not being naive. I told you, this isn't all on you. I was praying all night, and I think, just like you, that this is a good plan. I trust God to keep me safe. Unless you can tell me the plan works better without me at the subway station, and unless you know a safe place I can hide where I won't go crazy waiting to hear from you, I want to be there.

"This person, this mole, has hurt my son. He hurt Toby and Dale, and the people at the hospital. I want to help take him down. You said a good cop doesn't let distractions stop him from thinking objectively. Won't you be able to focus on what's happening at the subway station better if you're not worried about what's going on with me somewhere else? Can you honestly tell me my being at the subway station won't help lure the mole out?"

Ben couldn't answer Alice.

This was exactly why he avoided entanglements. Other men might be able to separate their personal and work affairs more effectively, but he wasn't one of them.

He should be able to objectively assess whether the risk of Alice being abducted by the mole or gang if she was hiding nearby was greater than the risk of losing the mole if she wasn't at the subway station. It should be a matter of risk assessment and percentages. The main objectives were to identify the mole and ensure Chris's testimony could go forward.

But honestly, all he could think of was the risk to Alice. Would he function better with her hidden away where he wouldn't know what was happening to her versus having her near him where he could actively guard her, but where she might be in more danger as bait?

His ability to make sound judgments as a good cop was compromised, which compromised her safety. If he knew for sure there was another cop he could call, one who would not report him, he might be seriously tempted to pass this off to someone else.

Unfortunately, he couldn't count on any other man's loyalty after he'd knocked out the security guard, a former cop. That had been a hard line to cross, and any cop, any good cop, would want to contain Ben first and get explanations after. He couldn't risk that.

He couldn't be sure he'd have the time to explain. This was his worst nightmare happening in real life. And Alice was the one at risk.

He could see how much he'd upset her by planning to leave her out. And while her feelings shouldn't even factor in this decision he had to make, they did. Her feelings clouded up what should be a straightforward analysis.

He didn't know the right call here. And he had to make it on his own. Throughout his body, his muscles tensed, ready for action, as the potential outcomes ran through his mind.

Finally, he gave in. He decided if he couldn't trust himself, he'd trust her and God. She'd been right that they'd been lucky. Maybe it wasn't luck. Maybe it was divine providence. They could certainly use some more of whatever it was. And selfishly, he wanted to be near her.

"Okay, you're right. I don't like this, but if you really want to expose yourself to risk like this…"

Alice's face lit up with surprise and happiness. It was an extreme reaction for being allowed to put herself in danger.

Allowed. He suddenly understood that for her, being accepted as an equal partner was important. He didn't think it was something she was used to.

She wasn't a child. She deserved to have a say in something that was life and death for her. He had to… relinquish control.

"Thank you, Ben. I'll do what you ask. I don't want to be left out, to not know what's going on. And I really think I can help by being there."

The warmth of the look she gave him eased his tension. He was happy that he'd caused it. He was way past being objective when it came to this woman. He hoped God would take care of the both of them.

They assessed the clothing Alice had found on the boat. Ben could tell the cold was getting through Alice's lightweight jacket, so he convinced her to put on the oversized foul weather jacket they'd found and to wrap the scarf around her face. Right now, no one could tell that Alice was a woman unless they took a second look. Ben almost couldn't recognize her himself.

He put on one of the other hats from the boat stash and pulled it low over his ears. If anyone had pictures from the arena of the two of them, he wasn't greatly changed, but his stubble had grown in, and with the hat pulled low on his brow, he looked different.

He hoped it would be enough to get them to Rosedale. In the light of day, it would be much more difficult getting around than it had been for them last night in the dark.

They stopped at a coffee shop, took turns using the bathroom and then got coffees and donuts with some of their dwindling cash. They sat at a corner table, doing their best to look inconspicuous. The coffee warmed him up from the inside, and the caffeine awakened his brain. Alice regained some color in her cheeks, peeping over the man's scarf she had pulled down so that she could eat and drink.

Ben was sitting against the wall so that anyone walking by wouldn't see anything but the bulky shape of Alice in the chair across from him. This meant his face was visible, but he could also see if there was any interest in them.

Like every decision they had made up until now, there were risks and benefits to consider. There was no television in the shop, and no one spared them a glance. Most people were in a hurry to get to work.

Alice finished her donut with evident enjoyment.

Ben passed her a napkin to wipe off her fingers and leaned forward. "It's rush hour now. Transit is going to be packed. It should be good cover. We can take a bus up to the subway and then head west. Get out at Bloor and take one stop north."

Her eyes scanned his face, tension tightening the muscles in her cheeks and chin. "Are we not going to be together?"

"They're looking for two people. Let's try to stay close, but not with each other.

"If we get split up, and in these crowds, we could, we'll meet on the walkway over the tracks at Rosedale. Then I'll call in, giving each department only a fifteen-minute lead-up before the time you're supposed to arrive."

Her eyes closed. He wondered if she were praying. She probably was. And for some reason, it calmed him.

He reached over and gripped her hand. "I'm still not sure I like it. I'm trusting your God to get us there and to keep you safe. But, if you prefer, I'd be happy to try to hide you somewhere."

She opened her eyes, and there was no fear there.

"I like having you beside me, but you're right. *I can do all things through Christ which strengthenth me.*"

Ben remembered that verse. He clung to it as they stood and made their way out of the coffee shop. Alice stood at the bus stop while he walked ahead to the next one. He knew she was praying. For her sake, and for his, he hoped God was listening and would take care of her, because he didn't even want to think about anything bad happening to her.

NINETEEN

Alice would like to say that she felt no fear as she stepped on the bus to the subway. It was already so crowded that it was standing-room only, and she could barely make her way halfway to the back before the other people already hanging on straps and seat backs made the aisle too congested for her to go any farther.

She wasn't terrified, but she was nervous. There was a constant, *Help me, Lord!* going on in the back of her head as the bus pulled out from the stop. It was a shock to remember that not quite twenty-four hours ago, she'd been hiding in her closet. She relaxed slightly when she saw Ben out of the corner of her eye as he made his way onto the bus at the next stop. She kept her gaze out the window, watching the dingy snowbanks pass by.

It was a gray day. The clouds were low, threatening snow. Part of her mind noted that the temperatures should warm up.

The bus lurched, and she was jostled into the knees of the person sitting on the aisle seat next to her.

"Sorry," she said.

The woman nodded and kept reading her book, but

Alice saw a cross on a necklace around the woman's neck. Alice pulled in a breath. She wasn't alone, even though she and Ben weren't together. God was watching over them. She knew people were probably praying for her back home. They might not be praying for exactly what she needed at the moment, but they were praying, and God would provide the help they needed.

Chris would be praying, too. And she took a moment to ask her Father to watch over her son and the others who would worry about her. Then she gave herself into His hands. *Not my will, but Thine.*

When they reached the subway station, Ben got off before her, and she lost sight of him as the crowd pressed into the station. Still, that calm was with her, and she let the crowd push her onto the subway platform, heading west. Many of the commuters were dressed in business attire under their coats. She knew she looked frumpy and disheveled, but everyone was wrapped up in their own concerns, paying no attention.

There were frumpy, poor and homeless people everywhere. No one wanted to make eye contact. These commuters were more likely to notice her if she were wearing expensive name-brand clothing, the kind they would want themselves. There might be safety in frumpy.

When she glanced up at the display monitor, checking to see when the next train would arrive, she caught a glimpse of her and Ben's faces on the screen as the content flipped over. It startled her, disturbing her calm, but she reminded herself, *I can do all things*, and then the subway train pulled in beside her, and the crowd flowed into the car, sweeping her with them.

She saw a glimpse of Ben's hat at the far end of the car and knew he was still with her.

All the seats were taken again, so she stood and hung onto a strap. There was nothing to see out the windows except the dark walls of the tunnel flickering past, and when she looked around at the rest of the people in the car with her, no one was paying her attention. No one had noticed their pictures on the display monitor and recognized them. It was reassuring. Of course, if Ben had really abducted her, the same lack of interest would have been terrible.

At Bloor Station, almost everyone in the car poured out the doors. Alice went with the flow and paused when she had some space to look for signs to direct her north to Rosedale Station.

She knew she had to switch from the east–west line to the north–south one, which was up one level, but she needed to be sure she arrived on the right side of the tracks.

On this level, the trains in both directions spilled out their passengers into a central aisle with escalators, stairs and elevators moving people from there to the upper level where the north–south subways cars ran.

On that level, the trains ran down the middle of the station. There was no central platform offering access to commuters going in both directions.

The only way to get on the northbound train was to be on the platform on that side. If she made a mistake and arrived on the southbound platform, she'd have to turn around and come back down to this level to get to the right stairs.

It would take time and might draw attention to herself, which was the last thing she wanted. It might mean she'd miss the train Ben was on, and she knew that would worry him. It wasn't what she wanted, either. She finally saw the stairs marking the north tracks and headed that way.

Alice paused at the foot of the stairway, mouth dry when she saw a police officer at the head of the stairs, scanning the bodies working their way up. She was shoved forward by the crowd. She tucked her hat down and stared at her feet, moving up one step at a time, ignoring the policewoman as she was swept along with the other travelers. She tensed her shoulders, heart rate jumping as she waited for the woman to shout something or to grab her arm.

Nothing. The crowd pressed on, and Alice followed like a lemming heading to a cliff. Soon, she stood on the platform waiting for a northbound car. She finally accepted that she hadn't been recognized. Maybe the policewoman wasn't even looking for her.

Still, tremors flicked through her body as she waited, more exposed now that she was on the platform. The majority of the rush-hour crowd wasn't heading north. Of the many bodies who'd been on the stairs with her, most had climbed up to street level and out of the station, off to their jobs, or shopping, or whatever they were doing this morning. There were only a few people waiting for a train with her. She glanced around and didn't see Ben.

She had a moment of panic and turned, determined to find him, when the northbound train rumbled toward her. She froze. Should she head to Rosedale or wait for Ben?

She really, really wanted to wait for him. Her gaze

swept over the station again. It was mostly empty on this side. Commuters filled the other side as the people there waited for their train.

She heard the chime of the doors of the car in front of her as they readied to close. She was the only one left standing on this side of the platform. She leaped forward, barely making it into the car before the doors slid shut. She sat on a bench, feeling lonelier and more exposed than she had since this whole debacle began.

Ben watched Alice head up the north stairs. He wanted to give her a good head start so that no one realized they were together. Then he saw the police officer standing at the top of the stairs.

He recognized her. He'd helped train her. No way would she not recognize him. Not if she was here to look for him. Before he could pull back into the crowd, her gaze caught his. He saw recognition and shock cross her face. She quickly reached for her radio, and he knew he had to vanish, fast.

She started down the stairs toward him, and he turned back to the subway trains. There was an eastbound train sitting there, and he slipped on board. He headed toward the back, and through the windows, he caught a glimpse of the police officer headed toward the train.

He continued toward the back of the train. He couldn't see her any longer because of how the platform was structured. He heard the chimes of the doors starting to close again, and he slipped out and rounded the corner of one of the walls that made the platform narrow. As the train slipped by, he saw the female police officer on the train staring at him.

He didn't have much time. She'd have problems communicating with other officers on the underground of the subway, but she could pull the emergency cord. He raced to the stairs, his rushing not unexpected among the commuters. Some frowns were directed his way, but he ignored them.

Once on the next level, the one with the north–south trains, he went for the nearest exit that took him to street level. He slowed his pace to the quick walk other people were employing on the sidewalk.

Rosedale was only one stop north. His best chance to get there without being spotted was to walk. It was still cold, but the exercise would keep him warm.

He hoped Alice got to the station and waited for him. He picked up the pace, staying at a walk, his anxiety pushing him forward briskly.

He needed to get to Rosedale before the mole.

So he did something he hadn't done for years. He prayed.

His eyes were open and his head was raised, but inside, he pleaded, *Keep her safe. Don't let me do anything to mess this up. I don't care about me, but she deserves to get through this.*

Help us. It was a mantra that underscored every step, every breath.

It felt like an eternity but couldn't have been more than ten minutes when he arrived at Rosedale Station. He had enough change in his pocket to pay for admission. He'd tensed, afraid his picture would be broadcast here, too, but with the busy morning rush, the agent at the window barely glanced at him before quickly focusing on helping the person behind him.

Ben headed up the stairs to the station proper. There

was a slowing herd of bodies heading through the turn-stiles and over the walkway to the southbound trains. He headed to the walkway himself, watching for Alice. He caught something out of the corner of his eye, and there she was. The relief was so overwhelming that he caught himself offering up a prayer of thanks before he was aware of it.

She was standing in front of the subway map as if trying to find her way, but her gaze was flicking over to the walkway.

He took a couple of steps and stood beside her. He saw her start, and then noticed how she relaxed when she recognized him.

She let out a breath. "I'm so happy to see you."

He loved that. He loved that she was happy to see him. But he wished it weren't just because he was her refuge right now. He reminded himself he was a cop, and she wasn't interested in having any kind of rela-tionship with a cop.

Right now, he needed to focus on being the best cop he could be. A cop who wasn't handicapped by caring too much for the person he was protecting.

"I'm happy to see you, too. I'm going to step into that corner there and make my calls. Can you look busy?"

"I'll head down to the north line, forget something and come back up."

He looked at her, wanting to argue that she should stay where he could see her, but he knew that wasn't the best call.

"Be careful."

She nodded. "You, too." She turned and walked away without asking why he'd taken a detour on his way to join her here. She didn't ask why he hadn't been on the same train as her. She trusted him completely.

He could not mess this up.

Once she was safely out of sight and heading down the stairs, he pulled out his phone and turned it on for the first time in almost a day. He ignored the messages and notifications that lit up the screen.

After this many years on the force, he knew people both in homicide and witness protection. He had carefully chosen the two people he'd call.

"This is Ben Parsons. I don't have time to explain, so here's what's happening. There's a leak in the department, which is why I've gone AWOL. I'm taking precautions. I'm bringing Alice Benoit to the Rosedale Subway Station. In fifteen minutes, I need a couple of uniforms on the northbound platform to provide protection. If I see anything funny, we're gone."

He hung up and made another call. This time he was careful to say they would be on the southbound station, then he hung up and turned the phone off again.

Fifteen minutes left no time to make elaborate plans. His message was short, and they wouldn't have time to track his location from his phone. There'd be no time for the mole to realize Ben had called a second person. Ben was counting on the fact that the mole would need to come up with a plan on the fly and would therefore make mistakes.

He saw Alice coming back up the stairs. Her gaze met his, and he nodded. Together, they headed toward the walkway over the train lines. In just fifteen minutes, they would know if their plan had worked and Alice would be safe, or if he'd cost her everything.

TWENTY

The next fifteen minutes were the longest of Alice's life. That was saying something, considering how the last twenty-four hours had gone. She and Ben stood on the walkway, watching the subway trains coming and going.

They saw a uniform on the southbound platform first. She nudged Ben, and his gaze quickly followed hers. A second cop came through one of the platform entrances, and the two of them stood against the back wall. A train came in, and the two officers watched it. When no one approached them, they remained, ignoring the curious glances.

She leaned over. "So which department is following your orders there?"

"Witness protection."

Alice bit her lip. If Ben was right, that meant trouble would come on the northbound side, from someone in homicide.

Ben's expression was grim. She wondered if he knew many of the people working in homicide. Maybe he'd been hoping the mole was in witness protection.

Or maybe the mole hadn't been able to step in in time, and two more officers would show up on the other platform.

She glanced back at the southbound platform. The two uniformed police officers were still standing there waiting. There was no train in the station right now, so they were scanning the few people waiting for the next train, but they didn't appear anxious or alarmed. They were just doing their job, possibly expecting it was an exercise in futility.

Alice took note of their faces. She might need them soon.

She felt Ben stiffen beside her and turned to see why. He was staring at the northbound platform. She'd thought his expression grim before. Now, he appeared to be gripping his jaw so tightly that he might damage his teeth.

She followed his gaze, and saw a single man, stepping forward from the platform wall as a train came into the station heading north.

He was about the same age as Ben and was dressed in civvies, with a warm jacket over dress pants. He was watching the train just like the two uniformed police officers had, but his posture was less relaxed. Alice thought she saw his fist clenching as the passengers scattered.

The man checked his wrist, and then swung his glance around.

Another southbound train had pulled in, so he couldn't see the other platform. But his gaze swung up, connecting with Ben's. Alice almost felt that jolt herself.

The man looked over at her. There was something

in his gaze, some desperation, and it hit her like a cement truck. He was the mole.

He slipped back into the opening to the platform.

Ben had started to breathe heavily. He reached to pat his pocket. Alice guessed he had his gun there. Ben was no longer the man she'd slept against last night. He was a seasoned cop on a mission, and his expression was set in granite.

"You know him?" She didn't need his answer for confirmation.

He nodded.

"What's he going to do? What should we do?"

Ben's gaze was locked on the end of the walkway. He pushed Alice behind him and started moving backward.

"If anything happens, you run to those two uniforms. Understood?"

Alice nodded, but Ben's gaze was elsewhere. She forced out the word, "Understood."

"His name is Hanssen. You tell those two uniforms to take you directly to Lee—he's the guy I called in witness protection. Tell Lee that I have good reason to believe Hanssen is the mole, and don't leave Lee's side until you hear Hanssen is taken care of."

Alice understood his words. They made sense. But she'd only need to pass on that message if Ben weren't around to do it himself, and that idea petrified her.

They were in a public place. No one could really hurt them in a public place, right?

But the hospital had been public. Those men who'd driven into her protection detail hadn't worried about collateral damage.

The morning rush hour was over now, and they were almost the only people on the walkway. They were feet from the southbound access when the man in the jacket, the mole, appeared on the other end.

He dropped the hand he'd been holding up. In it was his badge. Alice was familiar with what that looked like. She understood he must have used his badge to keep everyone else back.

Now it was just the three of them.

"Ben. What have you been up to?" In his tone, Alice heard echoes of Henry chastising Chris for some child-hood indiscretion.

"You aren't getting her." Ben's voice was cold. Alice wanted to grab his jacket with her hand and hold onto him, but she didn't dare get in his way. She knew she had to let the professionals do their jobs.

Hanssen reached behind his back, and at the same time, she saw Ben reach for the gun he had under his jacket. Now, the two men faced off, each aiming their guns at the other.

Alice glanced around, desperately looking for help. There was nothing behind Hanssen, no one on the north platform. She looked behind her and saw the two cops on the southbound platform had noticed the standoff on the walkway.

They left the platform, undoubtedly on their way up here, but Alice's relief was short-lived. Whom would they listen to?

"You don't want any further blood on your hands, Hanssen. This has been too rushed. I called witness protection the same time I called you. Their guys are on the other platform. I don't know how you got here solo, but you can't keep this hidden."

"Oh, I think I can. When you're not here, I'll have time to implicate you."

The two were discussing this so clinically, as though lives didn't hang in the balance. Alice could only guess what Hanssen had planned. He'd probably shoot Ben and get the two constables to deal with him while he left with her. She was sure that would be the last anyone would see of her.

She couldn't let that happen. She didn't want to disappear, and she didn't want Ben shot. She shoved past Ben and stood between the two men, right in the line of fire. She had no fear for herself. Hanssen couldn't risk killing her. If she were dead, they would have no leverage with Chris.

It wasn't much of an advantage, but she'd use it.

She stared at Hanssen, the cop who was betraying his friends, his allies, his principles. She held a hand back, hoping it was enough to keep Ben from doing anything silly.

"You're not getting him. You won't dare shoot me, or my son will testify. That's the whole point, right?"

She moved closer to the mole, making sure he couldn't hurt Ben without hurting her.

The man shrugged. "As long as you're not fatally wounded…" he said and released the safety.

Ben could see Hanssen's decision in his eyes, and it galvanized him. He reached forward with his free hand, gripped the back of Alice's baggy jacket and shoved her down.

Everything moved in slow motion.

Alice lost her balance and started to fall. He heard the two police officers coming up from the north platform behind him announce themselves. He didn't bother with their words. Every bit of concentration and focus was on Hanssen.

Hanssen's finger pulled the trigger. Alice moved her hands back to brace herself as she fell. He pushed forward, in front of her. He saw people coming up behind Hanssen and knew that if he fired his own gun, he might hit someone else. The only safe weapon he had to use was his body.

He saw the slight jerk of Hanssen's gun, and part of his brain acknowledged that the other man had fired. Alice was on the floor, no longer in the line of fire. There was a moment of relief and then an explosion of pain in his chest.

He fell back like Alice had and the fire in his chest spread outward. Alice surged to her feet and ran forward. He wanted to tell her to run the other way, but his body was no longer responding to his commands.

Hanssen had dropped his arm, but as Alice charged him, he began to raise it again. Ben tried to call out to Alice, but it was too late.

Alice threw herself at Hanssen with her hands forward, shoving him back. Hanssen stumbled, obviously not expecting the blow, and his arms began to windmill. Ever so slowly, his body fell backward down the stairs. Then he was out of Ben's sight.

Alice paused for a moment, looking down beyond where Ben could see. The edges of his vision were growing black.

She turned and looked at him. Her eyes widened, and her mouth opened. She ran back his way, as the two officers knelt beside him. One was radioing for an ambulance, and the other was calling the station.

His vision narrowed further, and his eyes began to close, pulled down by invisible weights. The last thing he saw was Alice kneeling in front of him with tears in her eyes.

As his world went black, his last thought was that she was safe. With that, he relaxed into the dark.

Alice couldn't breathe. It wasn't possible. Ben couldn't be…gone.

One of the uniforms, the one who'd called for an ambulance, asked her to stand back. She choked back a laugh, realizing she was succumbing to shock, and that she needed to get control of herself. If Ben couldn't speak for them, she needed to. And quickly. There was still a lot riding on what was going to happen in these next few hours.

She pulled off her hat.

"I'm Alice Benoit, and this is Ben Parsons." She saw the officers react to at least one of those names. She had to make sure they reacted properly.

"Someone named Lee sent you, correct? To come here and get me from a southbound subway train?"

They looked at each other. They didn't answer, but the glance they shared told her she was right.

"Ben also called someone named Hanssen in homicide. He showed up without any support. He's the mole that's been leaking information about my son and me."

They didn't react to that.

"We've sent for an ambulance, ma'am. Can you stay here with my partner while I go look for the other man you mentioned?"

This wasn't good. Hanssen had fallen down the stairs and been knocked out. From the angle of one of his legs, she suspected he might have broken it. She'd wanted to make sure he was incapacitated and would no longer be a problem for them. That way she could help Ben. The police officer kneeling beside him had staunched the wound.

"Can you call Lee?" she asked him. "Please, I need to talk to him. I know I sound crazy, but I'm not. This really is a matter of life and death." She was on the verge of panicking when a calm feeling descended on her.

She drew in a breath. She wasn't alone, even if Ben couldn't help her, God could. She took a long breath.

She wasn't sure she'd convinced the officer, but something had. He placed a call with his free hand and passed her the phone.

"Is this the Lee that Ben Parsons called twenty minutes ago?" She couldn't believe how little time had passed. It felt like a lifetime.

"It is. This is Alice Benoit?"

"Yes. Do you know about my son?"

"I know he's been giving the men guarding him a difficult time. He doesn't want to leave for the courthouse until he hears from you. Can I patch you through?"

"In a moment. I need to tell you something, and you'll need to deal with it right away. At the same time Ben called you, he called homicide and told them that I was arriving on the northbound train."

She paused.

"Clever man," Lee responded. Alice realized she didn't know his rank, but he knew about Chris. She hoped he would be able to take care of things now.

"Someone named Hanssen showed up on that platform. He's the mole. He shot Ben—" Her voice caught, but she continued, "Your men have called an ambulance for Ben and Hanssen will probably also need one. I shoved him down some stairs and I think he broke something. I hope he's still there. Can you make sure Ben is treated properly? I know everyone believes he's done something wrong, but he's kept me safe. I don't want Hanssen to convince your men Ben is the bad guy."

She stopped, not sure her voice would keep working. She could feel the lingering remnants of that earlier calm, but she was nearing her limit.

"Pass the phone back to one of my officers," Lee said. "And stay close so I can have you patched through to Chris."

She passed the phone back and gripped Ben's hand tightly, watching him lie there so still.

Hold on, Ben. Watch over him, Father.

Next thing she knew, the phone was returned to her, and she clutched it in her free hand and raised it to her ear.

"Mom, is that you?"

A wave of relief hit her. "Yes, Chris, it's me. It's been a tricky twenty-four hours, but I'm here, and I'm safe. We've found the mole, so we're all safe now."

Looking down at Ben, she hoped she was telling the truth.

She heard Chris sigh over the connection.

"First hockey skates."

She blinked and then remembered. Their code.

"Your first Christmas. You weren't even a year old. Your dad was anxious to have the next NHL superstar on the ice."

She heard a laugh. "Poor Dad. He was disappointed, I'm afraid."

She shook her head. "No, Chris, you were never a disappointment. Not ever. Your dad would be so proud of what you're doing."

"Sounds like he'd be proud of what you've been doing, too."

Alice swallowed a laugh that verged on hysterical. "I think he'd be surprised by what I've done."

"I gotta go now, Mom. They want to move me. You're good, right?"

"I'm good. A little cold, but otherwise I'm perfectly fine. But if you have some prayers to spare, the man who has been keeping me safe was shot."

She thought she heard a gasp on the other end.

"I want to hear about this, but I gotta go. I'll be praying," he promised. "And I want to properly thank him when this is all over."

She passed the phone back and saw EMT personnel approaching. Reluctantly, she let Ben's hand go and stood back so they could do their work. Ben was so pale and there was so much blood.

They checked him over, and in no time they had him on a stretcher with an oxygen mask over his face. That was good. If they were treating him, that meant they thought they could save him. They hadn't given up on him. She wouldn't, either. She watched them carefully head down the steps on the south side with Ben, and she swallowed a lump in her throat.

He has to make it. He has to.

"Ma'am, can you come with us?"

The two officers who'd been sent to pick her up from the platform were standing beside her, protecting her from the crowds that had gathered.

There was nothing more she could do here. She wondered what had happened to Hanssen and realized she didn't much care. After twenty-four hours of tension, of hiding, running and panic, her body was done. She was shaky and on the verge of tears.

She could only pray for Ben and Chris and let the police officers take her where they wanted.

TWENTY-ONE

Ben grimaced. It didn't matter what position he chose, it hurt. He could take the pain. That was simply a matter of endurance. His frustration, however, was making him irritable. He hated being kept in the dark.

He was in the hospital after taking the bullet meant for Alice, and he'd survived. He needed to know that she had, as well.

He'd been interviewed after he was stabilized, and before they took him into surgery. He'd insisted, because he didn't want any risk for Alice. He needed to get his story out there. But he was out of surgery and in recovery, and no one would tell him what was going on.

He'd been hospitalized for a few days, but he was still too weak to do anything, which didn't help. The doctors had been more forthcoming than his coworkers, so he knew he'd make a full recovery in time. That time was going to be a little longer, since he wasn't a twenty-year-old anymore, but there should be no permanent damage. He just needed to rest and let his body heal.

Easy for them to say. Physically, there was nothing

to do but rest. His mind, however, was running in circles, trying to put together what clues he had.

There were no guards outside his door, so that was good. If they still thought he'd gone rogue, he'd have been guarded.

As far as he knew, Alice hadn't come by, and that was not good. Obviously, he wanted to know that she was safe.

If he were honest with himself, he wanted to see her again for reasons that had nothing to do with police work. He wondered if she hadn't come to see him because she couldn't, or because she didn't want to.

It had taken her only twenty-four hours to completely tear down his carefully curated assumptions and walls. He wondered if she felt the same way.

If only someone would tell him something. He unclenched his fists again. With nothing to do but achieve maximum frustration, his fists were clenching a lot.

He heard a cough in the doorway and opened his eyes. He hadn't even realized he'd closed them. He hated being this weak, this vulnerable. What he saw when he opened his eyes was enough to lift his spirits. Not Alice, but almost as good. Inspector Lee.

"I'm glad to see you." Ben's voice was a croak, and he cleared his throat.

Lee smiled. "And I'm glad to see you alive and kicking."

Ben felt an answering grin. "Not kicking yet, but they say I will be before long."

"I'm sure I'm on the list of people you want to kick for not coming in sooner, but I didn't want to come before I could tell you what was going on. You were on the most-wanted list for a while."

That removed Ben's smile. "That many people thought I'd gone rogue?"

"I didn't want to believe it, but something dirty was happening with Chris Benoit. You were off-grid with his mother, and you took a long time to reach out."

Before Ben could explain, Lee continued, "Now, I get it. I know you weren't sure whom you could trust. I'd never have suspected you, but then again, who would've thought Hanssen would work with the gang?"

"It was definitely Hanssen, then?"

Lee nodded. "His son was doing drugs and the gang scooped him up. That was the major pressure point. His daughter was accepted to Harvard, so he was feeling a financial pinch, as well. And his wife… She's left him now, but I think she had a part in it, too."

Ben closed his eyes. Caring for people had made Hanssen vulnerable. For the first time, a voice inside Ben's head argued that being vulnerable might be worth it. Even cops deserved to have people care for them, to have people to care for. Lee had a family, and he was good at his job.

"So do you want to know what happened with the Benoits?"

Ben opened his eyes again and tried not to reveal just how badly he wanted to know.

"Did Chris testify?"

Lee shook his head. "Didn't need to. As soon as that scumbag knew his guys hadn't been able to shake

Chris, he turned witness so fast it made some heads spin."

"He's really turning?"

"Turned. It's a done deal. Doesn't want to spend time in prison. To be fair, he's made a lot of enemies. He's now in witness protection, and we're scooping up high-level gang members left and right. The end result is that the only revenge the gang wants now is on him, so Chris is free. And Alice Benoit is, as well."

Ben's mood was improving dramatically. Alice wouldn't be going into witness protection with her son.

"That's great news."

Lee sat in the visitor chair that had yet to see use. "Mrs. Benoit is an impressive woman." Lee didn't need to tell Ben that. "After you passed out, she took over."

"Really?" The last recollection Ben had was Alice holding his hand with a worried expression on her face... He wasn't sure he should dwell on that.

Lee had a grin on his face. "Oh, yeah. She made the uniforms call me so that we'd know you weren't the cause of the trouble. She was adamant that everyone understand you're the only reason she's alive. She put Hanssen out of commission. He whacked his head after she shoved him down the stairs and was still out cold when I got there."

The smile was wiped from Lee's face when he mentioned Hanssen. A dirty cop was a nightmare for the rest of the force.

Lee shook his head. "Her account of events matches yours almost perfectly, except that she gives you more credit. You're free and clear and can go once the docs sign off on your release. SIU will want to talk to you, but it's just to wrap up their paperwork."

Ben sighed. He wasn't strong enough yet to be pushing for release.

Lee watched him with an amused glance. "We've kept Mrs. Benoit away from here until we could settle all this. She's back home now with her son."

Ben nodded that he understood. He did. As witnesses, he and Alice weren't supposed to have the chance to conspire together or influence each other's testimony in any way. And, of course, Ben understood she'd want to be with her son after everything they'd gone through. He just wished she could be here, too.

"But I understand she calls every day to see how you're doing."

Ben shot a glance at Lee, who was still smiling.

"The two of you had quite the adventure together. I'm sure you'll have lots to talk about once you're on your feet again."

Ben wished he could be sure that she wanted to see him again.

Alice twisted her lips as she considered the box in front of her.

Most of her possessions were in boxes right now, but this box wasn't for her. It was for Ben.

A care package. She'd been getting updates every day from the nurses and knew he had a long recovery in front of him. Since he'd taken care of her and probably saved her life, it seemed only thoughtful to make a gesture of gratitude.

She'd boxed up a couple of cans of beans, a toy boat

and a flashlight. She'd put in a pair of scissors, a razor and a T-shirt from the basketball team they hadn't watched play since they'd been too worried about their future during the game.

Was it too much? Too personal?

"Hey, Mom."

Alice slapped the top of the box down. This was not something she wanted to discuss with her son.

"Chris! Everything packed?"

There was a for-sale sign on the front lawn. She and Chris had finished packing up their personal items and the real estate agent would be staging the house for buyers soon.

He scratched the back of his neck. "How did I end up with so much junk?"

Alice smiled. "I think it's called being a pack rat."

Chris clutched his hands to his chest. "She jokes, after we were nearly torn apart."

Alice's smile dropped, and Chris caught her expression and stilled. "Too soon?"

It would always be too soon, but she nodded and let that suffice.

Chris dropped the box by the door. "You're good? No second thoughts?" He cocked his head as he waited for her response.

Alice carefully examined his face. She used to be able to read him like a book, but he was an adult now. He joked about what they'd been through, but these last few months had added a gravitas to him, and she wasn't always sure she saw the real Chris when she looked at him instead of the one he wanted her to see.

"Are you having second thoughts?" she asked in return.

Chris shook his head. "I'm ready to go. I just have this feeling like I'm abandoning you."

Alice crossed over to him and pulled him into a hug. She could remember reaching down to do this, but now he was taller than she was. Taller, stronger and capable, but she still wanted to protect him.

He was right. It was time for him to step out on his own.

"You're not abandoning me. You're leaving the nest. If you didn't do it on your own, I'd have to kick you out. And since I'm listing the house, I kind of am…"

Chris hugged her back. "Yeah, I feel so betrayed."

They pulled back. "Seriously, Mom, it's fine. But have you figured out what you're doing next?"

She hadn't. She just knew it was time to move on. She probably had many years left, and she didn't want to spend them living alone in this house in the middle of nowhere with nothing but memories to keep her company.

Not all the memories here were good. She hated that the attempted abduction still affected her, but she didn't feel safe here, not the way she had.

"Maybe you should start dating."

Alice felt her jaw drop, and she was sure she looked as shocked as she felt.

"What? I'm supposed to be telling *you* that and asking for grandchildren." No, on second thought, she wasn't ready for that quite yet.

"Don't worry, Mom. I've done some dating. No one you've met because it's never gotten serious. Don't worry about me. But you're still pretty young. I know Dad wouldn't mind."

Alice didn't know what Henry would think of her dating, but it was nice to hear Chris's opinion.

"What about that cop you were on the run with?"

Despite her best efforts, Alice felt her cheeks heating up. She could almost believe the box in front of her was broadcasting Ben's name.

"What about him?" she asked in a strangled voice.

"I heard he's a widower." Turning serious, Chris put a hand on her shoulder. "Not all cops are the same, Mom."

It was a day for shocks. Alice had never allowed her frustrations with Henry to show when Chris was around.

"What do you mean?"

Chris shrugged. "Dad was always a better cop than he was a dad. It's not a stretch to think he was probably the same as a husband."

"You never said anything," Alice stammered.

"I know you always came to every game and every recital, and Dad didn't. He always said it was because of work, but some of my friends had dads on the force, and theirs showed up. I used to get upset, but I didn't want to upset you. I finally figured out that was his problem, not mine.

"I've heard you talking about Ben, and you sound… interested."

Alice didn't like that she was this transparent, and she didn't want her son setting her up.

"Chris, Ben and I were only together for about a day, and a lot of that was spent on the run. We didn't have a lot of time to discuss many personal things. One of the things he did say was that he needed to be unencumbered to do his job well."

"Unencumbered?"

"He didn't use that exact word. But he had some experiences when he first started working that convinced him cops can be distracted by someone they care about. That it's better for some cops to only have their careers to focus on. In some ways, it sounds like Ben might be a lot like your dad."

Chris's face fell. "Sorry, Mom. But if he can't see that you're worth more than a job, then he's not the right guy for you, anyway."

Alice had never expected to be having this conversation with her son, but his support gave her a warm feeling inside. "Thanks, Chris. Oh, and by the way, don't try to set me up unless you want me to do the same for you."

Chris's eyes widened, and he held up his hands.

"Point taken. We will not get involved in each other's love lives."

"But if you do get serious about a girl, I want to meet her as soon as possible."

"We'll make a deal. I'll agree to that if you'll agree to introduce me to anyone you get serious about." With a cheeky grin, Chris left the kitchen, taking more of his boxes out to the truck they'd rented.

Alice had some things to put in storage, and Chris would take his stuff on to Toronto where he'd found an apartment to rent with some friends. He'd be back in classes this fall. His life was returning to normal.

Alice looked at the box in front of her. She shook

her head and picked it up to take to the truck. She wasn't going to send it.

Instead, she put three envelopes in her purse to mail on her next outing.

She was sending Rita, the hairdresser, payment for their haircuts, and an ample tip. She was also sending a letter to Peter Dawson, who she'd tracked down, to thank him and to offer repayment for the beans and use of his boat.

The last envelope was addressed to Ben. It paid him back the money they'd spent that day: transit fare, clothes and food. She had no way to repay him for the rest of the things he'd done, and she shouldn't try.

Ben had told her he couldn't do his job if he had any attachments. She'd obviously read too much into how close they'd been during that dramatic day. She hadn't heard anything from him now that she was no longer his responsibility.

She should be smart enough to listen to what he'd said. She'd spent more than twenty years supporting a husband who had focused more on his job than her. She couldn't do that again, which meant she needed to change how she was thinking about Ben.

TWENTY-TWO

Ben was finally being released from the hospital. He still had some rehab to do and wouldn't be allowed back on the force for a while. Once he was back to work, he'd be on desk duty. By the time he was clear for active duty, he'd be eligible for retirement.

He'd had a lot to think about during these weeks while he recovered. And in the quiet times, rather than mindlessly watch television, he'd requested a Bible to read. He'd also talked to a counselor, and this time he'd taken it seriously. Previously, he'd said what he needed to say in order to get back to his job as soon as possible. This time, he thought it was worth seeing if the counselor could help him. His life was changing, and it was time to make sure the changes were good ones. He was looking beyond his job for the first time in decades.

He was finally facing that his issues regarding Mort and Laura might involve more than guilt. He'd suffered two devastating losses. Keeping himself clear of attachments had been a way of protecting himself from pain. He needed to accept that he couldn't avoid pain without avoiding the good things, as well.

He was also gaining comfort from reading the Bible. He'd marked a passage from Ecclesiastes about there being a time for everything. A time to live and a time to die.

He felt that one. He could do everything in his power to keep people safe and save lives while on the job, but not everything that happened was his responsibility. He couldn't control everything. That burden wasn't all on him.

That reminded him of how Alice had tried to comfort him by telling him that she trusted God and believed that he was God's agent. She'd wanted him to know they weren't alone and everything wasn't all on him. He hadn't appreciated it at the time.

Letting go of that responsibility left him feeling lighter and younger. But in spite of that, he'd still decided it was time to retire.

When his job was all he had, retirement had been something to avoid. He was changing and ready to find more. He'd decided that he'd done his best to make things better for the people around him. Now it was time for him to focus on his own life. There were a lot of good cops out there. It wasn't all on him.

He wasn't sure what his future held, but he knew the first thing he had to do was talk to Alice.

Maybe he'd misread the connection between them. Maybe it had been a result of the circumstances they'd been thrown into during that dramatic day. He'd never thought it was possible to fall in love with someone that quickly, but he knew he had.

He wanted to explore a future with Alice. But to

do that, he needed to show her that he'd changed. He needed to prove she could be his priority.

If she didn't want that, didn't care for him, couldn't see herself ever caring for him, then he'd have to find something else. He had no idea what that would be, but God would show him.

He knew almost everything about Alice. He knew where she lived, where she'd worked, who her friends were. All that had been in the dossier he'd been given when he'd been assigned to keep an eye on her. But Alice wasn't part of a case he was working on for his job. This time, it was personal, and he didn't want to use that information about her to his advantage.

He didn't want to come to her as a cop. He wanted to come to her as a man who was interested in a woman. He'd wondered about showing up on her doorstep, or if he should call first. It was less daunting to use the phone, but what he wanted to say needed to be said in person. He needed to watch her face, see how she reacted, not just hear what she said.

He'd just made that decision when he received an invitation to return to the Lychford detachment for a party. Even though he hadn't been at the detachment long, and he'd been replaced for the rest of the supervisor's maternity leave, he was invited to a party being thrown to welcome that supervisor back from leave.

He accepted it as an indicator from God. Perhaps he was being naive, but he liked to think this was his time for love, and that the time to hate had passed. He accepted the invite and made sure to look his best when he drove out. If Alice wasn't there, he'd stop by her house after.

It was time for him to try to grab some happiness.

* * *

Alice didn't want to go to this party.

When Henry was alive, she'd attended every event that the detachment was involved with. It had been almost a duty. After he died, she'd thought she would be free of those obligations, but she couldn't completely cut herself off, because she was friends with many of the people who worked in the detachment and their families. She liked to spend time with them. She had cut back, though, and she was trying to make a new life for herself, one that didn't revolve around being a cop's wife.

The real estate agent was showing the house this afternoon, so she couldn't stay home. Chris had told her she should go. It might be the last time she would be in the area to go to one of them.

Reluctantly, she'd agreed to make an appearance. It wasn't that she didn't want to see her friends, but it was a small town, and everyone knew she had her house up for sale and had heard about the attempted abduction. Everyone wanted to ask her about it and know what she was planning to do next.

Alice also wanted to know what she was doing next. She'd prayed about it and talked to some of her friends, but she still didn't know.

She didn't want to stay in the house she'd lived in with Henry, and she didn't want to live out in the country on her own. Most people expected she'd find a small place in town, but she hadn't found anywhere that felt right yet. And she didn't know what she'd do in town. She'd been a teacher for years and had enjoyed it, but she didn't want to continue on with that.

She was unsettled. And she didn't like that part of that feeling was connected to Ben Parsons.

She knew he'd been released from the hospital and was probably back at work or would be soon. She also knew he liked her. There had been a connection between them, and she'd seen the warm look in his eyes.

If she reached out to him and they explored their connection, she'd be involved with a cop again, and she didn't want to do that.

Ben might not even be willing to risk an emotional involvement with her. In his eyes, a relationship would be another possible weak spot.

She knew it was probably best to ignore Ben and make her own plans, but somehow she wasn't able to do that. Despite common sense telling her it was impossible, she was afraid that it might be possible to fall in love in twenty-four hours, and that she might have done that with another cop.

She shook her head, locked her door behind her, checked her surroundings the way she always did now and got in her car to head to the party. Ironically, at least for a few hours, being at a party full of cops might distract her from a certain cop she was trying not to think about.

The supervisor's baby was cute, and his mom was glad to be back around the people she worked with. Alice was enjoying herself, despite frequently needing to tell people about her adventure in Toronto and that she had no plans yet. Even though this was a party for the new baby and his mom, Alice felt like the center of attention.

It was getting more difficult to repeat her story and say she still had no plans for her future all while smiling. She knew it came from a place of caring, but all the questions about what was next for her was making her more frustrated with her own indecision. Maybe she should just put a placard around her neck saying she just didn't know yet.

It was a beautiful spring day. It was still crisp and cool, but the snow was gone, and bits of green were springing up in the brown lawns and flower beds. Alice stepped outside for a break to get some fresh air and quiet. The room had been packed with people, and her strange malaise made her want to make her excuses soon and leave.

But then she'd have to go back to the house on her own, and that wasn't appealing, either. Her real estate agent had texted that the showing had gone well, but he had no other news.

She sat on a bench and took a long breath of fresh air.

"Alice?"

A shiver went down her spine when she heard someone say her name. For a moment, she thought she was hallucinating. How in the world could she be hearing Ben here? But then Ben stepped around the end of the bench, and she realized it wasn't a hallucination or a dream. It was Ben. The shiver spread throughout her body.

His hair was cut short, and he was smooth shaven. Drinking in his appearance, she noted that he'd lost weight and looked pale. Still, he was smiling, and she couldn't resist smiling back.

"Ben," she half whispered.

His smile grew, and he nodded at the seat beside her. "May I?"

She nodded. He settled beside her, and the faint scent of his aftershave tickled her nose. She gave herself a mental shake.

"You appear to be doing well. I'm so glad."

He shrugged. "Not a hundred percent yet, but I'm getting closer all the time. You look fully recovered."

Alice reached for one of the short curls that made up her new short hairstyle.

"Except for losing a few pounds of hair, I didn't have much to recover from."

She saw his gaze run over her face. "Spending time on the run like that can leave you with things other than bullet wounds to recover from."

Alice swallowed. "I'm still a little on edge. I'm jumpy when I hear things at the house, and I find myself looking for cars or people behind me...but I'm safe, and I know that. It will just take some time."

He examined her face with an intent look on his. "Is Chris with you?"

She shook her head. "Not anymore. He's gone back to Toronto."

Lines creased Ben's forehead. "You're completely on your own in the house? Are you good with that?"

She shrugged. "It's temporary. I've got the house listed, and there was a showing this afternoon."

Ben's eyes glinted. "Really? Have you decided where you're moving to?"

Alice shook her head. For some reason, it didn't

bother her when Ben asked her what she was going to do. She wanted Ben to be curious about her plans.

"I didn't want to commit to a place before the house is sold. And—" She paused, not sure how honest to be. She couldn't be totally honest. "I haven't decided what I'm going to do yet. But what about you? Are you really okay? Are you back to work?"

Ben took a moment before he answered. "Well, that's not a simple answer."

Ben had been thinking and dreaming of Alice since he'd last seen her. He'd thought he knew how he'd feel when he saw her again.

He'd been wrong.

He arrived late in Lychford. A truck had tipped over on the highway, so Ben had pulled into the parking lot fifteen minutes ago. He'd been greeted warmly by people he'd worked with for only a short time. People here knew what had happened. Alice and Chris were some of their own, and they were grateful that he'd taken care of them.

But while he'd answered greetings and maintained the social chitchat that politeness dictated, he'd looked for Alice. Once he'd finally spotted her, she'd slipped away, and that brief sighting had made his heart rate speed up.

He needed to see her, to talk with her. He didn't know how it had happened, but after spending that eventful twenty-four hours with her, he never wanted to spend another day without her.

He'd counted down the days of his recovery and started making big changes in his life. He'd also been praying a lot that Alice would give him a chance. Now, when she asked about work, it was the opportunity he'd been waiting for.

"I don't think I told you, but I'm almost eligible for retirement now."

She opened her mouth, hesitated, and then said, "No, you didn't mention that."

Of course, he hadn't. He hadn't been able to consider retirement at that point. He took a breath, because he was ready to take his chance.

"I didn't like to even think about it. Working was all I had. But I've had a lot of time to think these past few weeks."

"Ben, I'm sorry I didn't come to see you—"

He put a hand on hers where it rested on the bench. "Alice, it's okay."

Her hand tensed under his, but she didn't move it. She stared down at their fingers on the bench and bit her lip.

"I've had time for a lot of things. And one of them, thanks to you, was reacquainting myself with God."

That surprised her, and her gaze shot up to his.

He nodded. "Yeah, you got to me with your talk about someone looking out for us. And you were right. It was a difficult thing for me to accept at first. It made me revisit a painful part of my past. But I was able to look at it with a better perspective after all this time."

He looked out at the signs of life returning in front of him. Hopefully, it was a sign the same could happen in his own life.

"I was finally able to stop blaming myself and to recognize that not allowing people close to me was less about maintaining objectivity in my job, and more about protecting myself from pain."

He looked back at Alice. She was watching him intently, like she had a vested interest in his reevaluation of his life. He hoped she did.

"You and I were able to work together, and we found and captured the mole. And I wasn't objective in the least."

Her eyes widened at that.

"So now, I want more. I want more than just being a cop. I've got a couple months of desk work left, and then I'm starting a new chapter in my life, where I'm not going to be a cop."

Alice turned her head away, and her cheeks flushed. He wasn't sure how she felt about what he'd said, but there was only one way to find out.

"I'm still not objective about you, Alice Benoit. I'm hoping you might be willing to spend some time with a cop who's working a desk. If not, we can wait until the end of summer when I won't be a cop at all. Maybe together we can figure out what's next for both of us."

Ben stopped and swallowed the lump in his throat. Was that enough? He hadn't come right out and told her he'd fallen in love with her, but he didn't want to scare her off before she agreed to give him a chance.

The pause lengthened, and Ben fought the urge to fidget, but her hand was still under his, and he didn't want to give her an excuse to break that contact.

Alice finally spoke. She stared at the ground, but her words were encouraging. "Do you really think you can be happy if you're not a police officer, Ben? It's been your whole life for so long."

He squeezed her hand gently. "I haven't been on active duty for a few weeks now. I don't think I can sit around and do nothing, but the city has kept itself going without me. There are other good cops out there, and it's their turn. I'm ready to do something for me."

Alice looked at her feet as he watched her. Then she turned to look up at him.

"What do you think you'll do instead? Golf? Fishing?"

He kept his gaze on hers. "I'd give those a try…if I had someone to try them out with."

"Someone like…who?"

She was maintaining eye contact, and he thought her glance was happy, hopeful. It made him feel the same way.

"Well, it would have to be someone I could get along with. Obviously. Someone I could spend time with in small spaces. In difficult situations. Maybe even someone I could go to a basketball game with."

There was a whisper of a smile on her face.

"Maybe someone who could drive a car if you needed to keep your gun in hand?"

The fist of his free hand clenched. "I never want to be in a situation like that again. But it would be nice to know that whoever I'm with is able to keep her head in situations like that."

Alice took a long breath. "And if this someone perhaps wanted to be more than friends…" Her gaze had dropped again.

Ben used his free hand to reach for her chin and tilted her head up. "That would make the someone perfect for what I want."

"Really?" Alice whispered.

"Alice, can I finally kiss you?"

She moved her hand from his and shifted closer to him so that she could slide her palm up his chest and around his neck. "I thought you'd never ask."

It was a soft kiss, a gentle one, but it was full of promise.

Ben drew back, admiring the pink on Alice's cheeks, the sparkle in her eyes.

"Do you believe it's possible to fall in love in twenty-four hours?"

A smile picked up the corners of her lips. "To misquote a Bible verse…all things are possible."

"I love you, Alice. I love that you woke me up, made me see what I've been missing, showed me that God has been here with me the whole time. And I promise with all my heart that you're going to be my priority."

"I love you, too, Ben. I was worried about whether I could be involved with a policeman again, and I knew you didn't want any attachments."

He opened his mouth, and she pressed a finger to it, making him shiver.

"I've been praying about what's next for me. No answer came, and I was frustrated, but now I know. It's you."

Ben liked the sound of that. He wrapped his arm around Alice, finally able to do it as the man who loved her, the man she loved. This time, they weren't scared, and hungry, and freezing cold.

He didn't know what was next, just that they'd figure it all out together. God would lead them. And he could ask for nothing more.

* * * * *

Dear Reader:

Writers always ask, "What if…" Which leads our minds down sometimes unusual and unexpected pathways. For *Kidnap Threat*, the trail started when a Love Inspired Suspense editor expressed an interest in older characters and a different twist on witness protection. My mind came up with a widow, learning to her dismay that her university-aged son was in temporary witness protection, and due to a leak in the police department, she was exposed and now a target for the people her son was going to testify against.

An ordinary woman, suddenly caught up in danger, relying only on God and the man God sent to protect her. Alice, with only her courage and faith, in a situation that could even conceivably happen to me. I'm just not sure I'd handle things as well as Alice.

I hope you enjoy her story.

Anne

COMING NEXT MONTH FROM
Love Inspired Suspense

YUKON JUSTICE
Alaska K-9 Unit • by Dana Mentink
With her ruthless uncle sabotaging her family's reindeer ranch, K-9
team assistant Katie Kapowski heads home to help—and thrusts
herself into the crosshairs. She needs assistance, even if it comes in
the form of Alaska State Trooper Brayden Ford and his furry partner.
But with their rocky past, can they work together...and survive?

HIDING HIS HOLIDAY WITNESS
Justice Seekers • by Laura Scott
A frantic call from a witness whose safe house is breached
sends US marshal Slade Brooks to Robyn Lowry's side. But when
he reaches her, she doesn't remember him—or the crime she
witnessed. Now going off the grid until they figure out who leaked
her location is the only way to keep her alive...

YULETIDE COLD CASE COVER-UP
Cold Case Investigators • by Jessica R. Patch
When her sister's remains are found, cold case agent
Poppy Holliday is determined to solve the years-old murder.
But someone's willing to kill Poppy and her partner, Rhett Wallace,
to keep the truth hidden. And it's up to them to dig up the small
town's deadly secrets...without becoming the next victims.

HOLIDAY SUSPECT PURSUIT
by Katy Lee
After a murderer strikes, deputy Jett Butler and his search-and-
rescue dog must work with the sole witness—FBI agent
Nicole Harrington. But Nicole's the ex-fiancée he left behind after a
car accident gave him amnesia years ago. And unlocking his past
might be just as dangerous as facing the killer on their heels...

SMOKY MOUNTAIN AMBUSH
Smoky Mountain Defenders • by Karen Kirst
Someone wants Lindsey Snow dead by Christmas—and she doesn't
know why. The only person she can trust to help her is the man she
betrayed, mounted police officer Silver Williams. But can they figure
out who is trying to kill her...before the holidays turn lethal?

TEXAS CHRISTMAS REVENGE
by Connie Queen
Emergency dispatcher Brandi Callahan believes her missing sister's
dead—until she answers a 911 call from her. When the cryptic call
leads Brandi to a little boy just as bullets fly her way, she turns to her
ex, Rhett Kincaid. But can the Texas Ranger shield Brandi and the
child through Christmas?

**LOOK FOR THESE AND OTHER LOVE INSPIRED BOOKS WHEREVER
BOOKS ARE SOLD, INCLUDING MOST BOOKSTORES, SUPERMARKETS,
DISCOUNT STORES AND DRUGSTORES.**

Get 4 FREE REWARDS!

We'll send you 2 FREE Books plus 2 FREE Mystery Gifts.

Love Inspired Suspense books showcase how courage and optimism unite in stories of faith and love in the face of danger.

FREE Value Over **$20**

IF YOU ENJOYED THIS BOOK, DON'T MISS NEW EXTENDED-LENGTH NOVELS FROM LOVE INSPIRED!

In addition to the Love Inspired books you know and love, we're excited to introduce even more uplifting stories in a longer format, with more inspiring fresh starts and page-turning thrills!

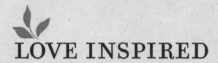

LOVE INSPIRED

Stories to uplift and inspire.

Fall in love with Love Inspired—inspirational and uplifting stories of faith and hope. Find strength and comfort in the bonds of friendship and community. Revel in the warmth of possibility, and the promise of new beginnings.

LOOK FOR THESE LOVE INSPIRED TITLES ONLINE AND IN THE BOOK DEPARTMENT OF YOUR FAVORITE RETAILER!

LITRADE0921